Earth Angel

A Fable

Tom McCann

Hot House Press
Cohasset, Massachusetts

For information about permission to reproduce
or transmit selections from this book in any form
or by any means, write to
Permissions, Hot House Press
760 Cushing Highway
Cohasset, MA 02025

This is a work of fiction. Names, characters, places and incidents either
are the product of the author's imagination or are used fictitiously.

Library of Congress Control Number: 2001099328
ISBN 0-9700476-1-4

Printed in the United States of America

Special thanks to Diana Donovan,
Peg Mavilia, and Sandra Goroff-Mailly

Hot House Press
760 Cushing Highway
Cohasset, MA 02025

For you . . .

CHAPTER ONE

The View from Below

There were almost twenty gallons of Sunoco unleaded on the ground. Will Wright didn't see the gas. He didn't smell it. He didn't feel it soaking through the soles of his work shoes.

Will wasn't the only one in Rockport that hot afternoon in August who couldn't take his eye off what was happening in the sky. But he was different from all the others. For one thing, he was the only one who had only one eye to watch with. For another, he was the only one watching the sky while overfilling the gas tank of the 1985 Ford Escort that belonged to Ida Brown.

People all over Cape Ann were looking up at a 1930 Stearman showing off as only a Stearman can in the hands of a skilled pilot. The pilot had started with loops—always a crowd pleaser—first inside loops and then the more difficult outside loops. Will knew that more pilots got killed doing outside loops than any other maneuver. Then came the spins, which thrilled the onlookers even more. Next, a series of hammerhead stalls, rolls, and graceful chandelles, ending with an Immelmann—not the most beautiful or graceful of all aerobatic stunts, but definitely one of the most difficult. Will was probably the only one watching who knew what an Immelmann was. He'd once done perfect Immelmanns.

Suddenly there was another plane—a 1960s jet fighter. It fell easily into place behind the Stearman, and chances were the Stearman's pilot heard the jet before he saw it. The jet began to mirror each move of the smaller plane, which now looked like a toy next to the larger, sleek, delta-winged silver warplane. After a few minutes the Stearman leveled off and slowed down, signaling that it was now the jet's turn to lead in this aerobatic dance.

The two planes segued stunts back and forth like two tap dancers on a stage, each trying to outperform the other. The onlookers below—from the lobstermen of Pigeon Cove to the sunburned tourists on Bearskin Neck—loved the impromptu show, and so did Will. But Will was watching it through a practiced eye—one that appreciated the fine-tuned skills needed to mimic a trick quickly and precisely. He allowed himself to reminisce momentarily on how he'd once flown like that . . . a long time ago.

Perhaps if Will Wright had had sight in two eyes, he might have seen out of the corner of one of them that Ida Brown's gas tank had been filled more than twenty gallons ago. There were other signs that could have told him the gas was spilling on the ground at the rate of one gallon every twenty-five seconds. Even so, he certainly should have smelled it. He should have felt it seeping through the hole in the sole of his left work boot. Or he should have heard the sound of the soft ding coming from the 1950s gas pump that announced each gallon. But he missed all the signs.

Suddenly, with the ground awash in gasoline and with Will still watching the show in the sky, a strong black hand came down hard on the nozzle and violently wrested it away from Will.

"Damn, mister, what are you tryin' to do, blow up all of Cape Ann?" the man said as he switched off the trigger of the pump.

"I'm sorry . . . I . . . I got a little distracted," Will said, startled and also very embarrassed.

"A little distracted? You weren't distracted, mister. I know what distracted is, and you were not it. What you were was totally shut down, that's what. You didn't hear the gas pump bells goin' off. You didn't smell the gas spillin' over. You didn't hear it hittin' the ground. You were standin' in a lake of gasoline. You still are. One spark and you'll be in another world and so will this lady in her ten-year-old car here, and maybe this whole place. What's with you?"

Will Wright ignored the tirade but was clearly embarrassed. Turning to Ida Brown and away from the stranger, he said, "This one's on us today, Miss Ida," Will said firmly, hoping to distract her from his mistake. "Ev—every thousand fills gets a free tankful, and you're the winner this week. Thank you for coming in, and you have a nice day now, Miss Ida." He picked up the water can he kept by the pumps for radiators that needed filling and began to pour some water over the wet gas on the side of her car.

"Why, thank you, Wilbur. That's so nice. You have a nice day, too. It is a lovely day, isn't it?" She

4

paused and then said carefully, "How are you doing, Wilbur?"

"I'm fine, Miss Ida. Just fine," he said politely, anxious for her to be on her way. But he wasn't "just fine," and he knew his sixth-grade school-teacher knew it.

"*Are* you all right, Wilbur? I hope so," she said, studying his face as he wiped the fender dry with paper towels from the dispenser. "I worry about you sometimes, Wilbur . . . out here all alone. Seems as if there are fewer customers every time I come here. I know it's real hard to make a living in your business these days, what with the big oil companies and what have you, and now here you are giving gasoline away. Are you sure you're not just being nice to your old teacher?"

"We're holding our own, Miss Ida . . . I'm okay." He set the can back beside the pump and checked to be sure the gas cap was on tightly.

"I often think about Casey, Wilbur . . . and Janet, too."

"So do I, Miss Ida . . . every day." Will hesitated for a moment, cleared his throat, and then quickly changed the subject. "You drive carefully now," he said, stepping back to give her room to drive off.

Ida Brown started her car and, with a nod to

the now-silent stranger, she slowly pulled away from the two short, rounded gas pumps that were showing signs of rust at the seams. Will looked after her for a few moments, then turned to the tall, black stranger who had picked up the water can and begun washing away the spilled gasoline. Despite the near miss and the cleanup to be done, Will stole a last quick look at the sky. Only the Stearman was there now, doing lazy eights.

"That other guy is probably over Connecticut by now. He headed southwest," said the stranger, who was considerably more in control of himself than he'd been just minutes before. "It looked to me like an old jet, but old or new it makes no difference. They can all still get up and go."

"I've seen that jet around here before. Once, about a year ago, that same jet came in real low right over the station here. It must be privately owned. There aren't any markings on it, so it's not military. They're selling off a lot of the old ones these days—"

Then he stopped himself and held out his hand. "I'm Will Wright. Thanks for your help."

"Benjamin Mapes." The stranger put down the water can and took Will's hand in his own. "I'm sorry I came on so strong, but it could have been . . .

6

well, you know. . . . This your place?"

"Well, that's my name up there," he pointed to the sign that said WRIGHT'S GARAGE, "but the bank owns most of it. And most everything else I've got." He moved the can back beside the pump. "I can finish this up now. I'll hose it down. Thanks for waking me up. Now, what can I do for you, Mr. Mapes? Run out of gas? Got a flat?"

"I got no car, but you might say I have run out of gas, and I'm definitely flat—flat broke, that is." Ben smiled faintly at his own humor. "I need a job for a few weeks until I get my bearin's and figure out where I go from here. I can fix engines . . . matter of fact, I'm good at it."

"Anybody who actually fixes engines nowadays is an endangered species," Will said wryly. "With everything being done by computer, only the dealers can fix 'em, or even tune 'em up. These days, pretty much all we do here is change oil, fix flats, and pump gas—and not too much of that—except when I get distracted like I did a few minutes ago," said Will, smiling slightly for the first time since they had started talking. Actually, it was the first time all day—and perhaps even longer than that.

"I don't have a job for you, Benjamin. I'm sorry, I just don't. I can maybe help you out with a few—"

He started to reach into his pocket and stopped. "Come to think of it, we do have Ellie Smith's sick Cat coming in here tomorrow. Ever work on a Caterpillar tractor?"

"Call me Ben. No, but I've worked on Abrams tanks and they're close. Just diesels, gears, hydraulics, and tracks, except for the armor and the guns."

"Vietnam?"

"Yeah," said Ben barely above a whisper.

"I think that one was the worst. Much worse than my war for a lot of reasons," said Will. The muscles in his jaw tightened as he looked away.

"Yeah, it was, but a few enterprisin' people in this country have already found a way to make a Broadway musical out of it and make a billion bucks. I hear they're makin' money off the war in Vietnam too: they've turned battle sites into tourist attractions. You can buy T-shirts that say I'VE WALKED ON THE HO CHI MINH TRAIL or buy pens made out of bullets or pay a dollar a bullet to shoot an AK-47 rifle," said Ben ruefully.

"Marines, Ben?" said Will, not wanting to pursue Ben's last comment but also not wanting to completely change the subject.

"No. Army."

Will thought for a minute. "I can go eight dollars an hour for as many hours as it takes, as long as it doesn't take more than ten or twelve. After that . . . well, after that it'll have to be over."

"That's fine," said Ben. "We'll get Ellie Smith's Cat purrin' again quick as we can."

Will noticed the bedroll and knapsack on Ben's back for the first time. "Over the barn there's a small room with a bed, a toilet, and a tin shower that will probably run rusty water for the first five minutes. Nothing fancy, but it's clean and the roof's tight, although it's not supposed to rain tonight. It's yours if you want it while you're here. I live in that little Cape in back of the station. You can take your meals with me for as long as you can stand it. I mostly cook eggs, open cans of soup, make sardine sandwiches, and eat a lot of takeout. Anything that comes in a paper carton—Chinese, Kentucky Fried Chicken, McDonald's."

"Sounds good."

Will wasn't sure why, but he found himself wanting to do more for this mournful-looking stranger. "If you need some walking-around money, I can let you have a small advance," he said.

"Thanks, but I have a few bucks, and, besides, I'm about walked out for a while." Gesturing toward the garage, Will said, "Well, why don't you get in a couple of hours now before we close? If you want to, you could help Joe—Joe Marino over there—with what he's working on. He'll give you a pair of coveralls."

And then, before Ben could reply, Will added, "Ben, there's one more thing. There aren't many rules around here, but here's one of them: the barn is locked," he said tersely. "It's off limits."

"Got it. I know about things bein' off limits." As soon as he said it, Will was sorry he did. His words sounded harsh and he felt that perhaps he'd come across too strong with the "off limits" remark, but that was the way it was, and he stifled the thought of an apology. Instead, he covered it by saying, "I'm glad to have you here, Ben. Maybe we'll get lucky and get another tractor or maybe an Abrams tank next week."

The two shook hands.

Will headed back to the pumps to finish the gasoline cleanup as best he could, and Ben walked toward the open bay. As Will watched him walk away, he realized for the first time since they'd met that Ben was black.

CHAPTER TWO

But for a Pebble

The first thing Ben saw when he walked into the single bay of the garage was a pair of legs beneath an old pickup truck on the ancient hydraulic lift.

"Hello," Ben said.

"I'm just snugging up the bolts on this here manifold, and it's a son of a gun. I'll be right with ya."

He assumed that the voice belonged to Joe Marino. "Take your time. I'll just take a look around." Ben was struck by how small and cramped the garage was. This was all of it: work area, tiny office, a single restroom, an old-fashioned mechanical cash register.

Most cars were a lot narrower in the days when this place was built, he thought. He noticed, too, that the inventory of fan belts, oil filters, and wind-shield wipers was very low—a sure sign that business wasn't good. The walls of the garage were full of airplane memorabilia: World War II posters; an assortment of photos, some in frames, some just thumbtacked up, including one of a very young Will Wright in a skull-tight leather hat with cutouts for his ears and a dangling chin strap. He was standing next to a biplane, which Ben guessed was World War I vintage.

"Almost got it," Joe called out through a grunt. Ben glanced out the open door toward the pumps. Will was still hosing down the spilled gas. At the same time he was looking up at the sky, at a new contrail left by a high-flying commercial jet as it had streaked across the sky heading east over the Atlantic on its way to some city in Europe.

There he goes again, Ben thought.

"Jeez, I'm glad that's over," said Joe Marino as he came out from under the pickup truck. He looked about seventy, the same age as Will appeared to be, and still going just as strong. "Ain't nothing older or dirtier than a thirty-year-old Cape Ann pickup, except maybe a forty-year-old Cape Ann pickup," he said, breathing heavily and wiping some of the grease from his hands. "Will's going to have to hose me down before I leave here tonight. Otherwise, Roseanne won't let me in the house. I'd shake your hand, but. . . ." He held up his grungy hands and smiled.

"Shake it anyway," said Ben, holding out his hand. "My name's Ben Mapes, and for the next couple of days, I'm the extra man who's gonna fix somebody's Caterpillar tractor. The boss told me to ask you for a pair of coveralls and see if I can help you."

"Well, I hope you're a forty-four regular, 'cause that's what me and Will are." Joe obviously enjoyed talking to strangers and friends alike. "Actually, he's a forty-two and I'm a forty-six, so we compromise on forty-four. Little big on him and a little small on me. That means we're both always a little uncomfortable but for different reasons, but it works for us. So forty-four's the only size we got."

"That'll be fine," said Ben. "Actually, it's been so long since I bought anything new, I don't know what size I am. Forty-four sounds about right."

Joe went to a metal cabinet and pulled out a pair of navy blue coveralls and handed them to Ben. "Hope you don't mind wearing a pair that says JOE over the pocket."

"Not if you don't." Ben motioned in Will's direction. "Known him long?"

"All my life. Sixty-something years. We went to grammar school together not more than five miles from here . . . halfway between Rockport and Gloucester—that's where I come from. Oldest fishing town in America."

Will, hose in hand, water running everywhere, was still looking upward. The white contrail was starting to break up into a faint dotted line. Ben asked, "What is it with him and airplanes? All this airplane stuff on the walls—and him always lookin' up at every one that passes by . . . like right now . . . at least it's a hose in his hand and not a gas pump. What is it about airplanes?"

"Just the way he is, mister. Everybody's got something. His something is airplanes. Mine's fixing thirty-year-old pickups. And yours seems to be asking a lot of questions. I hope you're as good at fixing diesels as you are at asking questions."

Ben ignored the dig. "Why airplanes?"

Joe Marino rubbed to loosen up his sixty-nine-year-old back and looked at Ben momentarily, wondering whether he should answer the question or tell this stranger to mind his own business. "He just loves 'em, that's why," he said impatiently.

"Comes by it naturally." He decided to explain. "Remember the Wright brothers—Orville and Wilbur?"

"Sure, a couple of bicycle mechanics who went on to invent a machine that would fly, and then they flew it."

"That's right, they *were* bicycle mechanics, and that sounds like a putdown to me. You might not know it, but it's almost always the bicycle mechanics and tinkerers of this world who come up with the big ones—the big inventions and discoveries—the Edisons, the Fords, and, yeah, the Wright brothers. Those are the guys—not the scientists and engineers—who come up with the blockbuster inventions. "And not only that, most of 'em are Americans, too. Go look it up in the encyclopedia and you'll see if I'm not right. And while you're at it, come back and tell me what the Japanese ever invented, as opposed to manufactured, or the—

"Remember this, it was amateurs who built the ark and professionals who built the *Titanic*, so don't go—"

"Hey, Joe, I'm not puttin' down the Wright brothers. I'm just sayin' what they were—bicycle mechanics. Lighten up, will ya?"

"Yeah, well, I didn't like the way you said what

you said. Anyway, his father named him after Wilbur Wright—Will's full name is Wilbur. Flying's in his blood. Was in his father's too; George Wright was the number-one man on Charles Lindbergh's famous flight team. George was a pilot, too, and he also did most of the engineering for that flight. He designed a lot of the special parts and equipment that went into modifying the *Spirit of St. Louis*—everything from the engine modifications to the special gas tanks that were crammed in all over the inside of that plane. Matter of fact, most of them were machined right here in Rockport over at the Cape Ann Tool Company in Pigeon Cove. It's closed down now— no more call for what they made. Building is still there, and the old machinery's just rusting away in the salt air."

"Did Will ever fly?"

"He sure did. His father taught him when he was twelve. Soloed at thirteen. Youngest in America. Was giving lessons himself by the time he was sixteen. He taught guys to fly who later became airline pilots. One of 'em, Bob Smith, became chief pilot for American Airlines in Boston—a Rockport boy, too. Anyway, Will joined the Army Air Corps the day after Pearl Harbor. It was a Monday. Graduated first in his class in flight school. Soloed the Stinson trainer after just two hours. And they were tricky things, too—tail drag-gers—you give 'em an inch too much rudder, and they ground-loop on you. That's an automatic washout . . . that's if you survive the crash. If you don't, they wash what's left of you off the runway. But Will was what the pilots call a natural flier. He was the best. Ever see the movie *Top Gun*? Well, Will Wright was a hundred times better. He could do anything with a P-51 Mustang. Anything."

"You talk like you've seen him do it."

"I didn't always pump gas and fix flats, mister."

Ben was beginning to realize that Joe's gruffness was just the way Joe talked and the best way to deal with him was to ignore it and simply go on. "Lookin' at him now, it's hard to imagine him a fighter pilot. I can't see him shootin' at anything. He looks like a fighter pilot—tall, slim, those sky-blue eyes, but he seems so . . . mild . . . so laid back."

"Yeah, he is that—laid back. I'd go so far as to say even shy—but believe me, underneath that mildness is steel and grit and a good heart and a brain that's . . . I didn't say he was a fighter pilot. What I said was that he was a pilot—and a good one. He never got a chance to be a fighter pilot.

Lousy luck. All his life Will's had lousy luck—Hand me that three-quarter socket wrench, will you? I need to give this thing another turn." He moved back under the car.

After a few grunts and a long pause, Joe continued. "I was there the day it happened. I'll never forget it. The cadets spent the morning shining everything themselves, their brass buttons and their airplanes. Graduation was in the afternoon. It was a clear, cool day. Everybody was turned out on the parade ground to see them. A hundred and fifty boys—and they were boys, too—just twenty-one, twenty-two years old, mostly. They threw out their chests and sucked in their stomachs when the commanding general pinned their silver wings right over their hearts and handed them their shiny gold lieutenant's bars. All kinds of brass hats were there—colonels, generals, guys in double-breasted blue suits from the War Department. Sweethearts were crying, some of the guys already had wives, others were getting married in the base chapel that afternoon after graduation, mothers with worried faces, proud fathers wishing it were them—but worrying all the same—aunts, uncles, kid brothers, all kinds of people. The planes were lined up wing to wing, and us ground-crew guys were lined up right behind them, standing at attention between the wing and the tail section. Not a cloud in the sky. . . ."

Ben began to pull on the coveralls but never took his eyes off Joe's face as the story continued.

"There was a lot of confidence in the air that day. You could feel it. We were at war and, by God, we were going to win. Sure, there was a lot of fear and tension, but it was a happy time too. Things were simpler and clearer in those days. You knew who the enemy was. On one side of the world there were guys who wore armbands and called themselves the master race and wanted to rule the world and make slaves out of all of us. On the other side there was a bunch of little yellow-bellied guys who started the whole thing with a sneak attack on Pearl Harbor. The whole country was united then. We were going to war and the country was going back to work again. And the women were great—'Rosie the Riveters,' they called 'em. They were building the planes our boys were flying. We could not have won the war without American women. Anyway, Will's graduation class was one of the first. Of course, nobody had any idea that in six months a lot of those same boys would be shot down, half of them killed, and a lot of them wounded or captured. Some people thought the whole thing'd be over in six months—especially the war with Japan."

"That's what they say about most wars," said Ben. "Over in six months. I don't think there ever was a war that some folks weren't sure would be over in six months. Years later, after millions of people have been killed, a bunch of guys in dark suits sit across a table and drink water that comes in fancy blue bottles—" He stopped abruptly. "Go on. What happened, Joe?" Ben continued to button up the coveralls.

"You wanna know what happened? I'll tell you what happened. Will was standing next to his plane. A brand-new P-51 Mustang that he named *Earth Angel*. He had Paul Strisik, the squadron artist, paint the face of Kate Hepburn on the cowling and under it the name *EARTH ANGEL*. That was the year the movie *Woman of the Year* came out. It was the first picture Spencer Tracy and Katharine Hepburn worked on together. Paul Strisik painted Kate wearing that big checkered hat she had on in the scene at Yankee Stadium. What a hat. What a face! She was beautiful. Will said she had the face of an angel sent to earth. And he named his plane *Earth Angel*.

"Anyway, there Will was, standing alongside *Earth Angel* and running his hand along the edge of her prop like pilots do—touching her lovingly and at the same time checking for any nicks that might have been caused by kicking up a stone on takeoff or landing. Slightest nick on a prop can throw it off balance, and first thing you know, you got serious engine problems, a runaway prop, or worse. Anyway, there he was, when all of a sudden he heard the plane next to him starting up and he instinctively turned to look at it. As he turned, the prop wash from that plane kicked up a stone . . . it wasn't even a stone, it was a damn pebble . . . but coming off the blade of that prop it had the force of a bullet. It hit Will Wright in the eye. Tore the eye right out of his head. I still get a shiver thinkin' about it.

"From that day to this, he's worn that black patch over it. He never flew a plane again. Oh, you can fly a plane with one eye. Just like you can fly with one arm or one leg. Wiley Post flew around the world and set a record and he only had one eye. And the legendary Colonel Arthur Metcalf, who lived right near here, in Winchester—a great pilot who had only one good eye. He flew everything from the Gypsy Moth to the B-52 bomber and the F-16. . . . But to be a combat pilot you need two eyes. In fact, they'd like you to have three—one in back of your head. Those guys have to keep looking from side to side and up and down. You just can't have a blind side in a fighter plane. Then there's the business of aiming the machine guns—six of 'em—and dropping the two six-hundred-pound underwing bombs. No, his days as a fighter pilot were over before they began.

"Anyway, the Army Air Corps offered him a desk job and the chance to keep his commission. But they didn't know Will. He turned that down. Said he'd rather be a mechanic. He wanted to be near the planes and the pilots who flew 'em. That's the way it is with people who love planes . . . even if they can't fly 'em, they want to be near 'em and the people who do fly 'em. So he and I worked together —fixing planes all over the Pacific—Wake, Midway, and Iwo."

"What happened after the war?"

"After the war, we both came back home to Cape Ann—him to Rockport, and me to Gloucester. I tried the family fishing business, but it wasn't for me. We both got married—him to Janet Baker, and me to Roseanne Russo. He was my best man. I was his. He bought this place in '47 with a GI loan, and

I came to work for him. Been here ever since. A lot else happened between then and now . . . " Joe Marino paused, then said, "Will Wright is the finest man I've ever met—a gentleman. Smartest, too. Ain't nothing he can't do or figure out how to do. Strongest, too. He's been through a lot but never once have I heard him complain about the cards he's been dealt. Not once. And God knows he's had plenty of reasons to. He's got character. I know that's an old-fashioned word these days, but Will has it."

After a moment Ben cleared his throat and said, "That's a sad story, Joe. Real sad."

"Yeah, it's sad, and it gets a lot sadder," Joe said, biting his lip and turning his attention to a flat tire that needed fixing. "Help me with this, will you?" he said, brushing a tear out of the corner of his eye with the cleanest part of the back of his hand, which wasn't very clean and left a long black smudge on his cheek.

CHAPTER THREE

Bad News in a Black Chevy

Any tire ripped over half an inch is considered by tire men to be a bad flat. This one was a bad flat, and they had to get the tire off the rim in order to examine the inner wall to see if it could be saved. Ben was putting downward pressure on the tire, and Joe was attempting to get the tire iron under the lip of it to separate it from the rim. They almost had it off when a late-model black Chevrolet sedan ran over the air hose that set off the alarm bell. On the car's door, in two-inch-high golden Times Roman letters, were the words CAPE ANN SAVINGS AND LOAN.

Will stopped counting the day's receipts and Ben and Joe stopped working on the flat. The slight frown that came over Will's face caused his eye patch to slip. Will adjusted it.

As he did so, a man stepped out of the car who, Joe muttered under his breath, was Sherwood Blake, the bank's new chief loan officer. One look at Sherwood Blake was all Ben needed. He'd known other Sherwood Blakes. If you were making a movie and wanted a mean-spirited, penny-pinching, not-too-bright, small-town banker, Central Casting would send you someone who looked and talked like Sherwood Blake. He had a way of holding his head back, pursing his lips and at the same time wrinkling his nose so that he looked as though he were always smelling something bad.

Will squared his shoulders, took a deep breath, and walked toward the car. "Hello, Woody. Don't tell me you have trouble with that new Chevy?"

"No. I have trouble with your loan, Mr. Goodwrench! And don't call me Woody. We're not in high school, God knows."

"Sorry, Sherwood."

"Mr. Blake, if you please . . . I'm here on official bank business, and it'll be better for both of us if we keep this formal. Is there someplace we can talk in private?"

"Sure there is, but I have no secrets from Joe, and this is our new man for a while, Ben Mapes."

Blake looked down at Ben's outstretched hand but didn't shake it. "A new employee? Really! The business about to go under, and you hire a new man? That sounds like something you would do. You should be out looking for a job yourself."

"What can I do for you . . . Mr.Blake?" Will said wearily. "I assume it's about my loan, and I plan to—"

Before Will could finish, Sherwood Blake interrupted. "I'm here to pick up the keys and the title to that plane of yours. It is about to pass to a new owner and, while we don't actually need the title, it will make it a lot easier to have it. So go get it for me now. They're coming for it day after tomorrow."

Will was stunned. "What do you mean, 'new owner'?"

"What do *you* mean, 'what do I mean'? Are you losing your memory, too? Don't you remember that three years ago you borrowed a substantial amount of money from the bank? Twenty thousand dollars. Frankly, if I'd had anything to say about it at the time, you never would have gotten it. But even Mr. Standish, that softhearted old fool, whom I've now replaced, required you to put up

27

some collateral. Most of your collateral is practically worthless: that shack out back you live in and this dump of a gas station, which is about to go under if it doesn't fall down first. You've been notified, twice now, that your loan has been in default for over a year and that we're foreclosing. Don't you read your mail, Wilbur Wright?

"We haven't been able to sell this so-called gas station. There haven't been any takers for any of the collateral except for that wreck of a plane of yours. We contacted some old airplane dealers and, to our utter amazement, we found a buyer right away. The buyer is paying thirty thousand dollars for it, sight unseen. Seems there are only a few like it left in the whole world; most of them are in museums, and the others are not for sale.

"You owe us twenty thousand dollars plus back interest plus late charges plus administrative costs, which brings it to about twenty-eight thousand. That means you'll come out with about two thousand dollars, and you get to keep your house, dump that it is, and even your fifteen-year-old Ford tow truck.

"We're doing you a big favor, Wilbur Wright. Think about it, and you'll realize I'm right."

"I can't let you take the plane, Sherwood. It's

not for sale. I need some more time. Please."

"What do you mean, it's not for sale and you can't let me take it? It's a done deal, mister. Don't you understand? It has already been sold. What we are talking about here is our taking possession under the law. Understand? There's no debate . . . it's over. Now go get the title, and stop wasting my time." Blake drew himself up to his full height, touched the knot of his striped tie, and checked to see that his suit jacket was buttoned, looking very pleased with the performance he had just delivered.

Joe stiffened and forgot the pain in his back. He took three quick steps toward Sherwood, and for the second time that day Ben's strong arm gripped another man's. Ben's hand on Joe's arm was just enough to cause him to break his stride and realize that punching Woody in the nose, or whatever else he had in mind, would only make things worse for Will.

"Who is this man who wants my plane? Maybe if I talk to him and tell him—"

Joe Marino could hardly bear the sneer on Sherwood Blake's face as Blake said, "Talk to him! You couldn't get within a quarter of a mile of him. You're a nobody. You're a washed-up, bankrupt, one-eyed grease monkey, that's what you are.

The man we're talking about is Skyros Rexus, the billionaire Greek businessman and international playboy. 'Sky King,' as they call him in the press."

"What does a man like that want with my plane?"

"It's not your plane anymore. Get that through your thick head. It's his plane now. We take possession the day after tomorrow, and he's sending a flatbed truck to pick it up on Friday."

"He could have any plane in the world—a jet, a 747. . . . He probably already has one. Why mine?"

"Boy, are you thick! You've breathed too many fumes or sniffed too much rubber cement, fixing all those flats. If you come out of this with two thousand bucks, I suggest you take a couple hundred of it and get your head examined.

"But if it will make you feel any better, your plane is just what he's been looking for. He's moving it to Atlantic City. He's going to hoist it up to the roof of his new gambling casino on the boardwalk. They tell me he's going to outline it in pink neon and put a few puffy neon clouds around it. He's also going to have some blinking neon dots coming from the guns on the wings to make it look like it's shooting. Your so-called plane, Mr. Wilbur Wright, is going to sit on top of *The Sky's the Limit* casino.

It'll be seen by millions of people. It'll be famous. It'll be—"

"Never!" said Will through clenched teeth as he took two steps closer to Blake. Ben began to see another side of his new boss—one he had not seen earlier.

"You'll get used to it. Now, about that title certificate—" said Blake in a noticeably lower voice, trying hard not to back up as Will got closer.

Will interrupted Blake in midsentence, sternly and with his jaw set. "I said never." He stepped closer to Blake. "She'll never be hoisted onto any roof of some Atlantic City casino outlined in neon lights. She's a plane with a proud history. She's not a sign! She'll never be humiliated. I will not let that happen." Will's voice rose slightly but noticeably with each sentence, and Sherwood Blake's Adams' apple bobbed up and down between his sharp chin and his heavily starched white collar. "Now you get out of here, Woody Blake, before I lose my temper. Get going, and fast!"

Will reached for the car door handle and tore the door open. With his other hand he pointed firmly toward the driver's seat.

Blake stepped back, blinking hard. Realizing that he had pushed Will too far, he said, "I—I'll go now, b-but I'll be back tomorrow with the Rockport police." He got into the car, closed the door, started the engine, and apparently feeling less threatened, he added, "That pile of junk better be ready to be towed. Remember, it's a done deal. It's not yours anymore. It belongs to somebody else now, and that somebody is Skyros Rexus—Sky King. You try to pull anything and you'll be sorry. He's rich and he's powerful and he's tough. He'll squash you like a bug."

Blake drove off and almost collided with a Hood milk truck.

Joe broke the silence. "I can get a second mortgage on my house and maybe get ten thousand, and—"

"I could never pay you back. Besides, you heard him say they've already sold her. I can't believe they'd do that."

"Not *they*, Will . . . *he* sold it. Woody Blake has always been envious of you. From the time we were all kids he—"

Will interrupted. "Shut down the pumps, will you, Joe? And put the 'Closed' sign in the window."

CHAPTER FOUR

Earth Angel . . . *and Ben's Story*

Ben climbed the steep wooden stairs on the side of the barn. Each step creaked under his weight and the entire staircase seemed to sway as he got closer to the top. He had a feeling he was the first one to use it in a long time and made a mental note that firming up its supports might be another project he could offer to do.

At the top of the stairs he reached for the knob on the door, turned it, and pushed. The door was swollen at the bottom and kept springing back as he pushed to open it. After a few tries, he gave it a slight kick and the door flew open on its creaking hinges. A rush of hot, attic-like dead air rushed past him and took his breath away as he momentarily stood in the doorway.

He stepped inside a small loft-type room with two dormers. Both the floor and the walls were made from the same wide boards. A couple of faded hooked rugs were on the floor and a thin coat of whitewash covered the walls. There was a single metal bed in the corner with a thin mattress on it, and next to the bed was an old painted chest of drawers. In the opposite corner was a small sink mounted on the wall, a toilet partitioned off with plywood to make a rustic-looking stall, and the old tin shower Will had mentioned.

Ben switched on a ceiling light in the center of the room and noticed an old Arvin radio in a brown Bakelite case on the painted wood nightstand. He turned it on, half expecting to get '50s news or music. The dial instantly lit up to a soft yellow glow and Ben heard loud static, but that was all. He shut it off.

In the corner was a bookcase full of boys' books, a few model airplanes hanging from the bare-wood vaulted ceiling, a gray baseball bat with a large red R on the crown hanging from a nail, a hockey stick with CASEY lettered crudely on the handle in half-inch black electrical tape.

Ben sat down on the side of the bed and, after a

minute or two, pulled off his boots, put his feet up, and rested his head on the thin, musty, striped pillow. He thought about the events of the day—up at dawn, rolling his bedroll as he had done thousands of times, the three rides he hitched to get from Springfield to Boston, and then the two that took him up here to Cape Ann—his destination and a place he hoped would give him some answers, or at least some clues to the puzzle he was determined to solve.

He thought about Will and Miss Ida Brown and about what Joe Marino had told him: about Sky King and Sherwood Blake and the plane he and Will had talked about. Ben closed his eyes . . . for just a few minutes.

The noise came from below and woke him with a start. Since Vietnam, twenty-nine years earlier, he'd been a light sleeper. The room was in total darkness, and for a few seconds he didn't know where he was. Lying there in the silence that followed the noise, he did remember, and just when he had convinced himself that he might have dreamed the noise, he heard it again.

He sat up, put his feet over the side of the bed, instinctively picked up the Louisville Slugger nearby, and tiptoed out of the room and down the outside stairs. They creaked on the way down, just as they had on the way up, which Ben knew wasn't much help if there was an intruder in the barn.

Once he reached the bottom, he stopped and then quietly made his way around to the front. The barn doors were ajar a few inches, letting out a narrow shaft of blue light. Ben moved toward the light and looked in. He was stunned by what he saw.

There, bathed in blue spotlights, gleamed the most beautiful airplane he had ever seen. It didn't look real. Its fuselage was so polished, it looked more like chrome than the thin-rolled steel it was. Its vibrant blue trim made it look iridescent. Ben didn't know it then, but he was just a few feet away from an eleven-foot Hamilton four-blade propeller that had once cut through all kinds of weather, enemy flak, and other dangers that could have sent the plane crashing to earth. Behind the prop was the giant cowling that took up almost half the length of the plane and had space enough to house a 1500-horsepower Packard Merlin engine—three times the size of a car engine. The teardrop-shaped Plexiglas canopy rose behind the cowling. Directly under the cockpit was a giant air scoop to cool the engine. The undercarriage of

the plane curved up gracefully where the fuselage narrowed, and then flared into a delicate
tail. He was looking at a perfectly preserved P-51
Mustang.

His eyes went back to the front of the plane. On
the cowling was the painting of Katharine Hepburn.
She had on the wide-brimmed hat, the checked
suit, and the long matching gloves that Joe had
described earlier. Her chin was resting on her
hand, one eyebrow a little higher than the other, a
slight smile on her face—the bemused expression
she always wore whenever she looked at Spencer
Tracy, the man she had loved on screen and off.
Under the picture were painted the words *EARTH
ANGEL.*

Ben was so struck by the beauty of the plane
that at first he didn't notice Will Wright standing in
the shadows, down near the tail section, gently
moving the rudder from side to side on its long
piano-type hinge the way pilots always do in their
preflight check. As Ben silently watched, Will
circled the plane, lovingly touching every part of it
with the tips of his fingers. He lightly traced the
outline of the wings, moved his hands over the
edges of the blades of the giant prop, around the
cone-shaped prop cover, then over the cowling, the

fuselage, and finally back to the tail section. After making a full circle around the plane, he stepped back and looked at it in full view. Then he walked over to the small desk in the corner of the hangar and sat down in the old oak swivel chair.

Over the desk was a gallery of photos, a larger collection than the one in the garage. Ben could see them clearly. Some were of a young Will Wright as an air cadet. In other frames were Will's wings, his two gold second lieutenant's bars, and his pilot's certification from the Army Air Corps. On a wall hook was an old flight jacket, a battered Army Air Corps. hat, and other airplane memorabilia. What looked like an honorable discharge was in another frame, although at that distance Ben couldn't see for sure what it was. It looked exactly like the one Ben had received more than twenty years later. Next to that was a faded photo of Will with a young woman—Janet Baker, Ben assumed, because there was another one of her next to it. In that photo Janet had her wedding dress on, and she was smiling up at Will, who looked very young and very serious. There were other photos, including one of Will and Jan with a young boy on a tricycle.

Will Wright seemed to study the photos as if

seeing them for the first time. After a few minutes he buried his face in his hands; his shoulders shook slightly, and at that moment Ben wished he hadn't heard the noise that had brought him downstairs.

Ben turned and was about to tiptoe out when Will stood up and turned off the blue spotlights on *Earth Angel,* climbed up on the wing and into the cockpit. He settled into the seat and adjusted the shoulder harness. He reached out and threw a toggle switch, and Ben heard a low whirring sound as the master switch activated the gyros and the electric fuel pump. The green lights of the instrument panel illuminated Will's face, and in that light Will looked thirty years younger—more like the cadet in the picture on the wall than the aging, troubled man Ben had said goodnight to a few hours earlier.

Will left the cockpit's canopy open, the way pilots do for ventilation when they are going through their checklist and "run-up." Ben heard Will begin calling out a series of instrument and system checks, as he had probably done a thousand times before: "Master switch . . . on. Altimeter . . . set . . . zero-two-five. Flaps . . . normal. Left aileron . . . check. Right aileron . . . check. Left rudder . . . right rudder . . . controls . . . free. Rotating beacon . . . on. Electric fuel pump . . . on. Mixture . . . rich. Throttle . . . back. Ignition . . . on." Each time he spoke, something happened . . . a kind of response. Sometimes it was a click, sometimes a hum, other times it was a squeal or a light, sometimes it was a movement on the outside of the plane. The ailerons moved, the rotating beacon came on, and the rudder moved from left to right. Ben was startled by Will's sudden and loud shout of, "Clear!"—the pilot's warning to anyone outside the plane that the engine was about to be started and they should stay well clear of the prop. Then, "Ignition," and the engine started up with a roar and the massive prop began to turn—but slowly, like one of those ceiling fans in Rick's Place in *Casablanca*. The prop was obviously feathered, the brakes set and the engine throttled back, since the plane was not pulled forward.

Ben was astonished at all of this, but even more surprised by the fact that, somehow, he could see and hear most of what was being said in the cockpit. He could hardly believe what he heard next.

"All right, mister. Taxi out to runway two-two-L, hold, and let the tower know when you are in position."

Ben couldn't hear any response, but it seemed to him as though Will could. And he was right.

Will did hear the voice, just as he had heard it hundreds of times before:

"Roger, Captain. Two-two-L. I will hold and squawk the tower," Will heard Casey's young voice reply from the seat in back of him.

"Watch that ground traffic on your right, mister," commanded Will.

"Yes, sir. Had it in sight, sir," the voice replied to Will.

"Keep that head swiveling, mister. You're looking for other traffic. The Lord didn't give us eyes in the backs of our heads, but a pilot needs them there, so keep it swiveling."

"Yes, sir," said Casey.

"Coming up on two-two-L," reminded Will. And then he continued, "Wright-Patterson Tower, this is P-51 *Earth Angel* taxiing into position at two-two-L. I have a student pilot at the controls. We are doing our run-up and holding. Requesting permission to take off on two-two-L when cleared and to proceed on a heading of one-three-zero."

"Roger, *Earth Angel*," Will heard a voice from the tower reply. "Cleared for takeoff, two-two-L. Maintain heading two-two-five to two thousand feet, and then proceed to a course of one-three-zero. Over."

"*Earth Angel* rolling. Thank you, Tower. Good day, sir."

"Happy landing, *Earth Angel*." Will heard the tower voice over the roar of the engine at full power.

"That's it, mister," Will said as he closed the canopy just before takeoff. "Give her full power. Watch that prop torque. Don't let her pull too far over; she will, if you let her. Compensate with the rudder and keep her right on the center line. Good. Good. Now gently ease back on the stick. Don't jerk it. Easy. Treat her gently. She knows what to do better than we do. She wants to fly and will fly all by herself if you let her. That's it. You're off . . . you're airborne. As soon as you clear the end of the runway, bring your gear up. Don't put any drag on this lady."

"Clear of runway. Gear up, sir," Casey said. Will smiled approvingly.

"Watch your rate of climb and keep her wings steady and level. Good. At two thousand gently turn to your assigned heading. And remember to keep that head of yours moving. I don't see it moving enough. You've got to watch your back. You're not always going to have your old flight instructor with you to remind you."

"Yes, sir, I'll remember. . . . But we'll always be together, Dad . . . I mean, er, sir—"

At that moment the wind came up and caught the barn door. It blew completely open with a loud, high-pitched squeak of its hinges. Will heard it. The spell was broken. Will Wright sensed that someone else was there.

He flipped the latch on the teardrop-shaped bubble canopy of the P-51. "Who's there? That you, Woody? I told you to. . . ." He shut the engine off. The prop stopped instantly and all the systems shut down as Will climbed out of the cockpit and onto the wing. He looked in the direction of the barn door.

"No, it's me, Ben Mapes," Ben said, moving to the center of the doorway with the baseball bat still in his hand. "I was upstairs and heard a noise coming from down here. I thought it might be the guy from the bank or one of his repo men. . . . The door was open. I didn't mean to . . . I know this place is off limits."

Ben could see the anger in Will's eye and the color rise in his face. His body seemed to grow taller, stronger, and straighter. For a moment it seemed as if he might actually lose control.

Ben instinctively dropped the bat and advanced

the few steps to where Will was standing. Ben put a hand on Will's shoulder. Will's anger left as quickly as it had come.

"It's okay," Will replied wearily. "It doesn't matter. It's just that this is my private place. There's a lot of history here. It's been a tough day. First Miss Ida's car, her mentioning Casey and Jan, Woody Blake's visit . . . too much in one day for a tired old man who's running on the rims." Will paused for what seemed like a long time. He seemed twenty or thirty years older than he had looked when sitting in the cockpit.

"I used to come out here a lot with my son. I actually taught him how to fly on this plane. When it came time for him to fly a plane that could really fly, he just got in and flew it. He'd done it all before in the thousands of hours we spent doing it out here in *Earth Angel*.

"I come here a lot now. It makes me feel close to him to think about all those imaginary flights we took together. Sometimes I think I can still hear his voice just as if he were in the cockpit with me. He and I lived for the day when we'd actually go up together in her, but . . . " Will's voice cracked and a tear rolled down his cheek.

"You okay, Will?"

"I'm sorry." He looked away, then said, "I haven't cried in a long time."

"Nothin' to be sorry about, Will. Everybody cries when things get to be too much. I do, and I don't know anyone who doesn't cry sometimes. There's a lot to cry about in this world. A lot of sadness. A lot of tragedy. When I cry, the tears dry on my face and sometimes the salt in them leaves white lines running down this black face. How'd you white folks like it if every time you cried, you had black lines runnin' down your white faces?"

Will smiled, which was what Ben was hoping for.

"You white folks get all the breaks. You can cry and nobody ever has to know. We cry, and it's written all over our faces, so to speak. My grandma used to say it's healthy to cry. It's lettin' somethin' out of you so you can start fresh again until the next time you have to let somethin' out. My grandma was quite a special lady. I miss her every day of my life. She was the sweetest lady I ever met. She raised me when my mamma, her daughter, died."

Will studied Ben's face for a moment . . . and he looked into the saddest eyes he had ever seen. "Who are you, Ben?"

Ben hesitated for several seconds before he

45

answered. "I'm just a guy, Will. A drifter. A guy with no roots. A guy with nothin' to show for all the years he's spent on earth. A guy with a past. A guy who has no future. A guy who has pretty much run out of gas . . . run out of road."

"Are you running? Did you do something?" Will asked.

"Yes, I am runnin'. But not runnin' from anyone, just runnin' from myself and some bad memories. And not havin' much luck gettin' away from myself or those memories."

"How long have you been running?"

"Twenty-nine years come this March."

"That's a long time. Want to tell me what happened twenty-nine years ago?" Then he added, "You don't have to if you don't want to, Ben."

After a long pause Ben said, "A thing called My Lai happened. I was one of a hundred and five soldiers of Charlie Company, Eleventh Brigade, who walked into a small village called My Lai." Ben averted Will's eyes as he spoke. "In four hours Charlie Company slaughtered five hundred and four women, children, and old men. When we were done, we dumped their bodies in ditches. It was one of the ugliest days in the history of the human race and the history of our country. I can't get the sight of women trying to protect their babies out of my mind. I can't get the screams of children out of my ears. I can't get the smell of sun-hot blood mixed with our gunpowder out of my nostrils.

"I've been told that the Vietnamese have turned My Lai into somethin' of a theme park, with a cemetery, museum, storytellers, and a memorial that reads FOREVER HATE THE AMERICAN INVADERS. Big deal. The point is, only Calley got punished. My Lai is part of my past. Part of my present. It will always be with me . . . until the day I die."

"I don't know what to say, Ben, except that war does things to—"

Ben interrupted. "Nothin' to say. Nothin' to say or do."

Ben was right and Will knew it.

After a pause Will asked, "Did Joe tell you what this is all about?" He gestured toward the plane.

"Not exactly. He told me your father was a pilot and an engineer and he named you Wilbur Wright, after *the* Wilbur Wright. He told me you love airplanes. He told me how you got that patch over your eye, how he feels about you; he loves you, Will, and when you were out there hurtin' today, I

47

could see that he was hurtin' just as much."

Ben continued without taking a breath. "He told me a few other things too. . . . I assume this is the plane that guy from the bank was talking about. I don't know much about airplanes, but I recognize beauty when I see it and she sure is a beauty."

"This is *Earth Angel*," Will said, resting his hand gently on her wing. "They put her in my hands when she was just five hours old. We taught each other a lot about flying. I named her. I flew her. I fell in love with her and she with me. I know that. In the end, I had to give her over to another man and watch her go off to war. That was hard, although at the time I didn't know how hard hard can get. Anyway, I worried about her. Lost her. Found her again. Put her back together in every way but one."

"What's that?" Ben asked.

"She hasn't got her engine. When the war ended, she was abandoned on Okinawa. I tracked her down three years later in 1948. I found her at the end of a runway the jungle had reclaimed. She was rotting in a clump of twelve-foot-high, three-inch-thick bamboo—some of the bamboo had actually pushed its way through her wings and body. I cut her free. Took me three days of working until dark to get her clear. Aside from the battle scars and the fact that someone took out her engine, she was in good shape. Even her log was still intact. She saw a lot of action."

"No engine? But I just heard one, and saw the prop turn."

"That's a '47 Buick eight-cylinder, two-twenty-horsepower with a Dynaflo transmission in her—a car engine—just so I can turn on some lights—put on the rotating beacon, panel lights, use the radio, and turn the prop over. I designed and built a super supercharger that more than doubled the Buick engine's horsepower, but it's still far short of her original Allison engine's output." Will's voice lowered in embarrassment. "For almost fifty years I've been pretending she's still a plane. Pretending I'm still a pilot."

"Nothin' wrong with that."

"A man's got to stop pretending sometime, Ben."

"Why? If it keeps a memory alive and doesn't hurt anybody, why stop?" Softening his tone, Ben said, "Miss Ida mentioned Casey and Janet."

"Casey was killed in Vietnam in March of '68 . . . same year you were there. Actually, same month

49

as the My Lai. . . ." He caught himself before he used the word *massacre* to this man who was already having trouble living with his guilt. "He was flying a Phantom jet. A MIG shot him down." After a long pause Will continued.

"Casey was all we had. Losing him killed something in both of us. After he died, everything changed. Nothing seemed to matter as much as it once did. I always felt Jan blamed me for encouraging him to fly. She never said that, of course, but I think she did. Who wouldn't? I blamed myself. I still do.

"After a while we just stopped talking about it. We stopped talking about most everything. We both began to grow old faster than our friends did.

"One day Jan said she thought she should go back to be with her mother in Pennsylvania for a while." Will looked away and hesitated before continuing. "That was sixteen years ago. A few years later her mother died. She said she was going to stay awhile longer to settle things. We talked on the phone. We wrote each other occasionally. Then, the phone calls only came on holidays and birthdays—they were painful. We've known each other all our lives. We were very much in love. We were each other's best friend. You think it will be that way forever, and then something happens that makes you realize nothing is forever.

"When you're young you never think awful things can happen to you—they just happen to other people. Jan and I, well, there really isn't much more to say. . . . I haven't heard from her since last Christmas."

After a very long pause Will said, "As I said, Casey and I used to come out here a lot . . . almost every night. He loved it out here. So did I. He used to say, 'Someday, Dad, we're gonna dig up an engine for *Angel'*—that's what he called her—'and get her airborne . . . then we'll see what she can do. We'll do it—you'll see. You and me, Dad. You'll see.' Sometimes, like tonight, when I'm in the cockpit with the canopy closed and the real world outside, I can hear him saying those words and I'd swear he's still right there in the seat behind me."

CHAPTER FIVE

The Flight Plan

The two men stood in silence for a long time, not knowing what to say next, each pretending to be doing something—Will buffing a spot on *Earth Angel*'s wing with the sleeve of his blue denim shirt and Ben examining a fingernail as if looking for something wrong with it—the way men do when they don't know what to say next. After a while Ben reached into his back pocket and took out his worn black leather wallet. He didn't open it . . . just held it in his hand.

"Will," he said, "that day in My Lai—later that afternoon—word of what we did quickly got back to the Viet Cong, and they came lookin' for us. We had left the village and were halfway across a rice paddy when suddenly two North Vietnamese MIGs came out of nowhere, their machine guns and cannons blazin'. They were on us in an instant. There was no place to hide. I was sure I was goin' to die in the next few seconds, and after what happened that mornin', I didn't care. I just stood up and waited for the bullets to tear into me. I wanted to die.

"The others ran or fell down into the rice paddy. Some of our guys got hit on the first pass, includin' our platoon leader. I was just standin' there waitin' for them to make their second run. In a few seconds they were back. I watched as their tracer bullets hit a thousand yards in front of me, then came closer—a hundred yards . . . fifty—I knew my life would be over soon.

"Suddenly, there was another line of tracers at a right angle to the ones comin' at me. I looked up and saw they were comin' from one of our jets.

"One of the MIGs got hit right away and blew up over my head. The blast shook the ground under my feet. I felt my left eardrum burst from the concussion and the blood run down my neck. The other MIG and our guy went at each other. The MIG forgot about us—he was fightin' for his life. I've never seen anything like it.

"The guys who were left ran for cover in the

jungle. I still just stood there. I couldn't take my eyes off the battle goin' on above me. It was fierce. Both planes were riddled with bullet holes. You could see the pilots plainly when they made their low passes—sometimes only a couple of hundred feet off the ground.

"The MIG had the tip of one of his wings shot off, but he kept flying. They both climbed high, and somehow the MIG managed to get underneath our guy and hit him in the underbelly with a blast from his nose cannon. Our guy just rolled over on his back and stayed in that position in a big wide arc . . . on his back.

"He was almost right over me when his plane blew up. The explosion was like nothin' I've ever heard. Little pieces of the plane rained down all around me. Some were so hot they sizzled when they hit the muddy water of the rice paddy. When the larger pieces hit the water, a puff of steam rose up. An instant later the water of the rice paddy started bubblin' up.

"I looked up, and the MIG was gone. He was badly shot up, and I guess he headed for his home base or maybe even crashed. I don't know. Suddenly, it was quiet. Not a sound except for the gurglin' from the air bubbles bein' released from the downed jet.

"I started to walk out of the rice paddy to the tree line, but then I thought I saw somethin' surface in a cluster of bubbles. Somethin' white. It looked like a scrap of paper. I watched it disappear beneath the surface again, only to bubble up and reappear a few seconds later. That happened a few times, as though it just would not sink. I got the weirdest feelin' that someone below the surface wanted me to take it. I knew that was crazy, but still—

"The next time it surfaced, I moved closer and reached down and closed my hand around it."

Ben opened his wallet and took out a small piece of what had once been white paper, now creased and yellow with age. Will watched him unfold it carefully.

"You can see it's almost falling apart."

Will moved closer and saw that, handwritten on the paper, was a long column of two- and three-digit numbers with, here and there, a few letters. "What does it mean?" Will asked.

"That's what I've been trying to understand ever since that day," Ben replied. "Maybe nothin'. But I keep thinkin' it came from that Phantom jet. Where else could it have come from?

"At first, I thought it was the pilot's flight plan, that the numbers were his compass headings. Days later, when I got back to my base camp, I looked at some charts of the area with one of our chopper pilots, but none of the numbers had any meaning to me or to him.

"So I've just kept it all these years. I have a feelin' it's some kind of message for me and figure that someday its meanin' will become clear. After how it came to me, I won't ever let it go."

Will reached over and took the note out of Ben's hand, turned it over, and read aloud military style: "One-two-seven. One-two-eight. Zero-nine-zero. Seven-eight-seven. Seven-nine-zero. Zero-four-nine. Zero-six-nine. Zero-one-three. Zero-eight-one. . . ."

"Off and on I've tried to figure these numbers out. I felt it was important for some reason. The trouble was, I didn't know where to start from.

"Take the first headin', for instance. If you're in New York and set a course of one-two-seven, that's east, and you would be headin' out over the Atlantic Ocean for London. Or, if you are in Los Angeles and set a course of one-two-seven, you're still headin' east, and then how long do you go until you turn to the next headin', which is one-two-eight—only one degree away from one-two-seven? It doesn't make sense that a flight plan would change by only one degree."

"No, it doesn't. And look at the eighteenth heading—one-eight-zero. That's a one-eighty, and everybody knows a one-eighty is a turn back in the direction you just came from."

"Right. If this was a flight plan, you'd be flyin' all over the sky, and sometimes in circles. I tried to put it out of my mind, but I couldn't. Then I began to think it was some sort of riddle. One night a few months ago, in a kind of half sleep, it came to me that these are not compass headings at all—they're roads and highways. They're route numbers. So I've been hitchhikin' north, to where Route 127 begins—Rockport."

"My garage is near the end of Route 127."

"Yes, that's why I'm here. My plan was to spend enough time here to get a little travelin' money together, then follow 127 to the next road, which is Route 128, just five miles from here. Then to Route 90, Route 787, and so on.

"But what do I find here at Route 127? A pilot in trouble over his plane. A plane that deserves more respect than it would get surrounded by neon clouds on top of some money-grubbin' casino.

"Whoever wrote this must have been a pilot. He put a zero in front of the double-digit numbers because, as you know, that's the way pilots express compass headin's from zero to ninety-nine. Look at them on the road map here."

Ben unbuttoned two buttons from his blue denim shirt, reached in, and pulled out a tattered Esso road map. He spread out the map on the wing of *Earth Angel*. Tracing the routes with his index finger he said, "These take you from here in Rockport on Cape Ann, Massachusetts, to Alexandria Bay on the St. Lawrence River in upper New York State, then over to Cleveland, then to Chicago, then to Madison, Wisconsin, and then . . ."

"Then where?" asked Will. "There is no intersection from Madison to Route 290. . . . Wait a minute, 290 is a Texas highway. Look here."

"Yeah," said Ben, getting more excited now. "Galveston to San Antonio. Then there's that one-eight-zero—Route 180 to Galveston. Then 285 to Roswell, New Mexico, then zero-eight-two—Route 82—to where? Route 82 goes across the state of New Mexico. Places like Alamogordo. . . ."

"Or places like the White Sands testing grounds," said Will, "where they tested the nuclear bombs. Or the space center. Or Hollowman Air

Force Base. Why would anyone go there?"

"Will, I have a feelin' that the point is, we're not supposed to know where this journey ends."

"What about this notation before the Chicago routing, VA 1040, and then two numbers down, 12457941? Those are certainly not roads. And this one . . . just MR. Mister? Mister who?"

"I don't know," Ben said, looking at Will. "I've been tryin' to figure out those three lines for years. They sort of blow my theory that the numbers on the list are roads. But I've decided to follow 'em anyway, and maybe find out what they are when I get there." Ben paused and then continued. "There's a lot I don't know, but I do know I'm here in Rockport, where they begin, Will. I have a feelin' that this is what I'm supposed to do . . . that maybe there's somethin' at the end of it for me . . . some answers."

At that moment the same kind of a strong wind that had blown the barn door open slammed it shut. With the door closed in the windowless barn, Will and Ben could not see the massive bolt of lightning following the arrival of the wind. An instant later they were both startled by the loudest clap of thunder they'd ever heard. The thunder brought with it a steady downpour of rain that would test every roof in Rockport that night.

"Ben, maybe this is just the imagination of an old man, but hear me out: your arrival today . . . Woody Blake's threat to desecrate this plane that has served her country and that is the last place on earth I can be close to Casey . . . this road map. . . . Maybe all this is telling me that *Earth Angel*'s time in my barn has come to an end . . . telling me to take her away from here . . . to follow these instructions . . . take these routes wherever they take me. I think this slip of paper might be some sort of message. . . . Maybe from God."

"I don't know about it bein' from God. I don't even know if I believe in God anymore, but for the first time since this piece of paper floated down from the sky and landed in my hand, I feel that I'm close to findin' out why. If you want to move *Earth Angel*, take her along these routes or whatever else they may be, I guess I must be meant to go with you."

Distracted by his own thoughts, Will either ignored Ben's words or didn't hear them. "I have to leave tonight," he continued. "Joe can keep things going till I get back—Joe and you."

"Will, I'm goin' with you. I'm a part of this . . . have been for twenty-nine years. I have to see what this means, where it leads. Besides, you're goin' to need help."

"When I take *Earth Angel* away from here, she'll be stolen property and that will make me a thief. If you're with me, you'll be a thief, too, and I can't let you do that, Ben."

"You can't stop me, and besides, you're going out there on the road—and that's my territory."

CHAPTER SIX

Into the Night

They worked into the night. Hooking up a driveshaft from the Buick V-8 super, supercharged engine to *Earth Angel*'s wheels took the most time. That done, they loaded tools and then camping gear into *Earth Angel*—a tent, pots and pans, canned goods, flashlights, a first-aid kit, an AM/FM radio, road flares—everything they could think of that they might need. They stuffed as much as they could into the small baggage compartment and ammunition bays of the P-51.

They topped off *Earth Angel*'s huge gas tanks in the wings. Will tested the newly installed brake lights on either side of the horizontal stabilizer in the tail section. "She didn't survive the bullets and flak to end up on the roof of some gambling casino in Atlantic City outlined in neon lights," he said as he fastened his pickup's license plate to the tail and a WIDE LOAD sign above it. "We'll start out early."

"Captain, I think we should start tonight because those bank guys will be here in about thirty-six hours, and we need a good head start."

"Do you realize we'll have to taxi all the way to New Mexico?"

"It's not that far," Ben replied. "Especially not with a '47 super, supercharged Buick eight with a Dynaflo transmission under us."

"They're going to say we're crazy," Will said.

"Isn't that what they said about your namesake Wilbur, and his brother Orville? Just a couple of crazy bicycle mechanics who thought they were gonna fly." Ben smiled.

A few minutes before three a.m. and just seven hours since making the decision to drive *Earth Angel* away from Rockport and follow the flight plan, Will pushed her starter button. The propeller, powered by the fifty-year-old Buick engine, began turning. Ben opened the barn doors wide. It was still raining hard. Will released the parking brake and pushed the throttle forward. *Earth Angel*'s wheels began to turn slowly, then faster.

The three of them drove off into the night, and the rain beat down on the plane's cockpit bubble and the lightning danced off her wing tips for the first time in almost fifty years.

CHAPTER SEVEN

A Heart for Angel

Ben and Will took *Earth Angel* onto the only road out of Rockport—the same road Ben had come in on eighteen hours earlier and the same as the first listing on Ben's paper—Route 127. At the Rockport-Gloucester boundary line they approached the sign that read LEAVING ROCKPORT, PLEASE COME AGAIN. As they passed the sign—just inches past it—Will and Ben noticed that the road became dry. There was no rain past the sign, no thunder, no lightning. The sky was clear and the stars were out.

Surprised, they checked the weather report on the radio. It had not rained in any of the other four Cape Ann towns that night, the announcer said, mystified. A check of the national weather records revealed that it hadn't rained anywhere else in the United States that night either. "The satellite photo for tonight shows a single thunderstorm cell over Rockport only, extending up into space beyond the satellite's ability to measure its height," the announcer said. "More later."

Ben and Will were silent, keeping their thoughts to themselves as they trundled across the bridge that connects Cape Ann to Massachusetts. Will suddenly realized that he hadn't crossed onto the mainland for many years. Not since the night he'd driven Casey into Boston twenty-nine years before to see the Celtics play the Philadelphia 76ers—with Bill Russell battling Wilt Chamberlain. Ever since Casey's death Will had not left the Cape, keeping to Rockport and Gloucester because all that really mattered to him was in his own barn.

He realized now that he had pretty much stopped living all those years. He thought of Janet, and how unfair that had been to her. She had grieved for Casey, too, and he hadn't been there for her, frozen as he was. For the second time that night tears streamed down his face as he thought of the woman he loved and how much he had hurt her at a time when she was already hurting so deeply. He could see her as clearly as if she were there in the plane, but with that almost grim look on her face that she'd worn in those first months after Casey's death—when she went about cleaning house, doing errands, without smiling but with fierce determination that she would somehow find her way back to her own life again. She had had to do that alone, without a husband to talk to, to cry with. Feeling the road vibrate beneath *Angel's* wheels, Will wondered if he could ever make that up to his wife.

They taxied along the breakdown lane of the Massachusetts Turnpike all night and by first light arrived at the New York State border. As they knew she would, *Earth Angel* created a sensation weaving in and out of traffic and startling drivers.

At around noon Will decided to pull off the road at a truck stop about five miles east of Albany for the rest of the day and start out fresh the next morning. They had been on the road for almost ten hours and awake for more than twenty-four.

"At the rate we went today," Will said, "it will take two, maybe three weeks to get to New Mexico. That is, if we don't get run over by a truck or get arrested. That was a close call with that Iowa Beef eighteen-wheeler near Stockbridge."

"Sure would be easier if we could find an airplane engine to fit her," Ben said. "We could put it in, fly her to New Mexico, and be there in a few hours."

"There are just two problems with that," said Will. "The first is that there is no P-51 Mustang engine to be had, not for any amount of money—even if we had the money. I spent years looking for one. Went all over the country chasing down leads. One time I took off in the tow truck to Florida to look at a P-51 engine I heard about. Well, I found it.

"The engine was in a lumber mill. They had it rigged up to run a thirty-six-inch circular saw to cut cypress lumber. They had all kinds of belts and pulleys hooked up to the crankshaft. Three of the cylinders had frozen up tight—choked to death on the heavy Sears motor oil they were feeding it. Half the parts had been replaced with jerry-rigged junk. The carburetor came out of an old tractor and the fuel pump was from one of those early Toyota Corollas. Can you believe a Japanese fuel pump in a P-51 Mustang? So the engine is one problem, and the other is that even if we got an engine someplace, who would fly her?"

"Any idea how many P-51s were made?" Ben said, ignoring the last question in an effort to concentrate on first things first—the need for an engine.

"Exactly nineteen thousand two hundred and thirty-nine were produced in five years. About ten years ago, I read that there were only seven of them still flying . . . probably down to two or three by now."

"All the more reason why we've got to get *Earth Angel* back in the air," Ben said as he turned back to his road map to see where they were going tomorrow.

After a few minutes Will said, "You know, I've been thinking about that engine. There was this pilot—Jackie Larson—at Wright-Patterson Field. Very cocky and self-assured, but a great pilot. A natural. Flew with the Flying Tigers in China before war was officially declared. I remember the brass saying that the only thing Jackie could never learn to do in an airplane was to fly in formation."

"Fly in formation? I thought that was the easy part."

"It is easy. All you have to do is look out to one side and keep your distance from the other guy's wing—sometimes only a few feet away. It wasn't that Jackie couldn't do it, it was that Jackie didn't want to. Just not a team player. You see people like that in every business—the professions, sports, the military—usually they don't last in an organization. You must have known people like that."

"Some, I guess, but not too many. Most people fit in somewhere. But what made you think of Larson now?"

"Well, in the early days of the war they had Jackie ferrying P-51s from the various factories where they were assembled to San Diego. It was a staging area, and from there they were flown in large formations to the South Pacific. On one of those solo ferrying missions to San Diego, Jackie developed a problem over the desert on the New Mexico/Arizona border and had to make an emergency landing in a blinding sandstorm. Jackie crash-landed and barely made it down, climbed out, and started walking across the desert. They found Jackie two days later, dehydrated, sunburned, and running a high fever. They never did find the plane. They figured it must have been completely covered up in the sandstorm. They searched a little, but there was a war going on and they didn't spend too much time looking. They never did find it."

"You mean somewhere in the desert of New Mexico there's a P-51 that's been buried for fifty years? Will, we gotta find this Jackie Larson. For all we know, Larson might have been shot down over Stuttgart or Saipan or even Vietnam. But assuming Jackie's alive and shows us where in the ten-thousand-square-mile stretch of sandy desert the P-51 is buried . . . we buy us a couple of shovels, and we dig it up. Sounds simple to me."

"My brother-in-law—Jan's brother, Charlie Baker—works for Veterans Affairs in Washington. I'm gonna call him and see if he can find out what happened to Jackie. It's a long shot, but we've got to try."

There are always a lot of phone booths at truck stops—most of them broken—but minutes later Will was in one that worked, talking to Charlie Baker while Ben rolled out his bedroll under the wing. All he saw, when he closed his eyes, was road.

"I know Jackie Larson's name must be there someplace in one of the VA computers. I also know it's against all the rules, but it's very important to me, Charlie. I'm at a pay phone just outside Albany. The number's 518-555-2879. I'll be here until you call me back." Before Charlie had a chance to say anything, Will hung up. He stretched out on the bench next to the phone and didn't hear anything until two hours later when the phone rang.

Will got it on the first ring.

"To begin with, Will, you're right, this does break a lot of rules. They're getting tough on privacy issues, so you've got to protect me on this and don't tell anyone where you got it. Your Jackie Larson is quite a character. Flew a hundred-thirty-eight missions in China with the Flying Tigers. Had to bail out of three planes, two of them P-40s and the third a P-51. Before all that, back in the States, Larson crash-landed a P-51 in a sandstorm in New Mexico on a ferry mission in '42. Discharged three months after V- J Day. Ask me why Jackie Larson never got promoted or decorated."

"I think I know—discipline?"

"You got it," said Charlie. "The file on Larson is as long as your arm. Absolutely wild. Disregard for rank, insubordination, dereliction of duty, drunkenness, hotdogging, freelancing—you name it, Jackie Larson did it. One incident involved losing a plane and endangering the lives of others and of the mission itself through sheer negligence. Jackie eventually became a spray pilot for a banana company in Honduras—United Fruit. Here at the VA we've had Jackie in our care on and off over the years. A lot of health problems, mostly alcohol related— some falling-down types of accidents, and two years ago the old liver finally blew out. As a matter of fact, we have Jackie again right now—this time for good. Terminal, Will. I'm sorry.

"Four weeks ago Jackie checked into VA Hospital number ten-forty—as in the IRS Form 1040—in Evanston, Illinois. We still have Jackie in our computer as a patient, but if you want to get in touch with Jackie Larson, you'd better hurry, Will. And remember: you never heard it from me."

"Thanks, Charlie."

"Will, it's none of my business, but you and Jan . . . you two should talk more. . . . Neither of you is getting any—"

"She's not ill, is she?"

"She's okay, but—"

"I know, Charlie. I'll call her . . . soon. . . . Tell her that for me. And that I love her, but something's come up that I have to take care of first."

Ben woke instantly when Will returned.

When Will finished telling him about Charlie Baker's news, Ben reached for the folded yellowed paper, carefully opened it, and said, "Now we know what VA 1040 means."

CHAPTER EIGHT

Jackie Larson

For the next three days they followed the routes on Ben's tattered piece of paper. They traveled over interstates that took them across New York State, up to Alexandria Bay on the St. Lawrence River, then west to Buffalo, down along Lake Erie to Cleveland, through northern Indiana, and into Illinois. They got very good at maneuvering *Earth Angel* in and out of traffic, but still had too many close calls. They also had one flat tire and even the thick, heavy-duty fan belt broke under the added strain.

Along the way, some drivers just stared, some waved, smiled, and gave a thumbs-up to the plane. More than one rubbed his eyes in disbelief. What surprised Will and Ben was that there was never a reaction from the scores of state troopers and local police who passed them on the roads—no reaction at all. It was almost as if they did not see *Earth Angel*. What relieved the men was that there were no radio reports on them either—they checked often. Apparently, Sky King had not yet started to look for them.

Chicago was Ben's hometown. He remembered where the veterans hospital in Evanston was, and helped navigate *Earth Angel* there without missing a single turn. They cautiously rolled down an alley only three inches wider than *Angel's* wingspan. Fortunately, the alley was empty of cars. At the end of the alley, there was the hospital parking lot.

"Do you always remember streets like this— down to the width, so you know ahead of time if an airplane will fit?" Will asked Ben.

"I was famous for my reconnoiterin' in Nam," Ben said mildly. "They always made me point man on patrol."

At the main desk of VA Hospital 1040, the guard directed them to the seventh floor. Minutes later they were standing in front of the nursing station and the head nurse on duty, First

Lieutenant Marian Crumley, USN.

"Your friend is very sick, Mr. Wright," she said stiffly. "You may go in for a brief visit, but we ask visitors not to tire a patient by staying too long. I'd prefer a maximum of thirty minutes. We also ask visitors not to say anything that might agitate the patient, because the energy one expends when one gets excited diminishes the effect of the painkillers and the other meds. Jackie Larson is an extremely difficult patient . . . but then, you gentlemen know that, being good friends."

"Yes . . . we'll be careful, Lieutenant," Will assured her.

Nurse Lieutenant Crumley directed them to room 712, down the south hall on the left. Will was just about to knock and push the door open when Ben reached out and stopped him.

"Look at the number directly under VA 1040, Will," he said as he handed Will the piece of once white paper he removed from his wallet.

Will looked down and saw "712."

The two looked at each other. Neither said anything.

Will knocked and opened the door.

There were two beds in the room, but only one was occupied. In it, eyes closed, ashen, tethered to several monitors, an IV, and a Foley catheter, was Jackie Larson. As they quietly entered the room, Jackie sensed their presence and opened her eyes.

Jackie Larson was a woman! All along Ben had assumed that Jackie was a man. Will never mentioned that fact. It just never came up.

"Who the hell are you two?" Jackie Larson said in a raspy voice, barely looking up at them. "You look like a couple of cops right out of that TV show. That's the way they pair cops these days, isn't it? One honkie, one spook? Everything's gotta be so politically correct these days. . . . What the hell's the name of that show?"

Before either could think of a reply she continued, "I can't remember anything these days. Can't do much of anything, either. Can't see. Can't pee. Can't—Go away. Can't you see I'm dying?" Jacqueline Larson turned her face away from her visitors and faced the green wall.

"We want to talk to you," said Ben, still recovering from the shock of seeing that Jackie was a woman and ignoring the racial slur. "We're not cops. And we know you're sick." Then he added sarcastically, "I'm glad to see that your eyes haven't been affected."

Turning her head back in their direction, she

snapped, "Well, I don't want to talk to you or anybody else. I'd love to throw you out, but as you can see—" She gestured to all that tied her down, then grumbled, "Since you insist, talk fast, and then get out of here. I could die any minute."

Will cleared his throat. "Jackie, my name is Will Wright and this is Benjamin Mapes. You and I met almost fifty years ago at Wright-Patterson Field. I was a mechanic."

Jackie squinted as she looked at Will, then nodded her head slightly. "Yeah, I remember you." Her voice warmed a little. "Actually, I remember the eye patch. You were a pilot, right? They said you were real good until—Yeah, I remember now. Funny how I can remember fifty years back but can't remember what I had for breakfast this morning. What do you want from me? It can't be any heavy lifting, and it can't take too long." She laughed harshly. "I'd offer you something to drink, but as you can see, what they give me to eat and drink comes in this plastic bottle . . . and it goes into this here other plastic bottle. I've had trouble with bottles all my life. What did you say your name was?"

"Will Wright, and this is Ben Mapes."

"You're not a bad-looking guy," she said to Will,

a little flirtatiously despite her condition and her age. "Where have you been for the past fifty years?"

"I got married. Bought a gas station after the war. Had a son. He became a pilot and was killed in Vietnam and—"

Jackie interrupted. "Tough break, but I'd give my . . . well, I would have given a lot to have flown one of them jets."

"And I'd give anything to have him back," Will shot back with an angry edge to his voice that Ben had never heard before—not even that first day in Rockport with Woody.

Jackie immediately realized her insensitivity and wanted to apologize, but years of gruffness from living and working in a man's world got in the way.

"Er, I'm sorry," Jackie managed, lowering her voice. "I'm sorry I said what I did about your son," she said awkwardly. "I never had a kid, but I can't think of anything sadder than having one and losing him. When I got back from China after my stint with Chennault and the Flying Tigers, I visited the father of a kid I'd watched go down in flames on the Burma Road. If I live to be a hundred, which obviously I won't, I'll never forget the look on that father's face."

"I'm sure your visit meant a lot to him," said Will, his anger subsiding. "One of Casey's fellow pilots came to see us, and somehow, just seeing him and knowing what Casey's last days were like made us feel closer to him."

"No, didn't have any kids, but I did have a husband once. . . . I couldn't keep him," Jackie said, drifting on to a new subject. "One day he just had enough of me and my problems—the booze, always itchy and having to go, never wanting to build a nest. He just walked out. A year later I got a piece of paper that said we were divorced. He was a great guy, and I think about him a lot."

Jackie paused, still looking away from the men. "Even after the divorce, he's kept in touch. . . . He lives in St. Louis and calls me here every other day. Someday he'll call and I won't be here. . . . He knows that, and I know it too.

"He wants to come visit me, but I won't let him see me like this. It would upset him too much. A couple of times he broke down on the phone and cried. He tried to hide it, but I could tell." She turned and looked into their eyes. "His crying makes me feel he still cares. I don't like him to cry, but I do. Does that make any sense?"

"It does to me, Ace," said Ben.

Jackie smiled faintly. "Ace," she muttered half under her breath. "Nobody's called me Ace in a long time. Feels good. I did put a few numbers up on the scoreboard with the Flying Tigers, you know." For a moment she looked younger and not quite as sick as she had just minutes before. "Then some brass hat in Washington, some fat armchair general, found out that Jackie Larson was Jacqueline Larson and it was all over. Women were nothing in those days."

Saying that must have triggered something in her because she looked directly at Ben and said, "Hey, I'm sorry I said what I said a few minutes ago . . . that 'spook' business . . . I didn't mean it. I have a big mouth and I often say mean things before I take the time to think. It's gotten me in trouble all my life. I really didn't mean to offend you."

"No offense taken," Ben said. "Please go on with your story. You were saying. . . . "

"Chennault had to send me back. Next thing I know, I'm in the Women's Air Force Service Pilots—a WASP—the all-woman outfit assigned to ferry planes to the quote, fighting men, unquote, and occasionally pull targets for their gunnery practice. Hell, it didn't matter to the old man—to General Chennault—that I was a woman. Or to the other Tigers. Or the Chinese on the ground whose lives we were saving. It—"

She was starting to get red in the face. Remembering what Lieutenant Crumley said about getting Jackie excited, Will said, "Jackie, we want to talk to you about a P-51 Mustang."

"Well, you've come to the right place. I know more about the P-51 than the guys who designed it because I flew it and they never did. I flew hundreds of 'em for thousands of hours. I did things with that plane that the book said shouldn't be done and some things they said couldn't be.

"I put those babies in power dives and pulled out when the book said the wings would fall off. They didn't. That was the sweetest airplane ever made. It was a pursuit plane, a reconnaissance plane, a fighter bomber, a ground attack—you name it, the P-51 could do it all. There has never been a finer plane than the P-51."

Talking about planes was animating Jackie in a way Will and Ben wouldn't have thought possible. They let her continue.

She spoke as though giving a lecture. Her voice grew stronger and she used her hands to demonstrate, as all pilots do. "For power it had a one-thousand-and-forty-horsepower Allison engine. Her wingspan was exactly thirty-seven feet, three and a half inches, from tip to tip. The length from spinner to tail was exactly thirty-one feet, eight inches. Height: twelve feet, four inches, from the ground to the top of that beautifully designed, teardrop-shaped bubble canopy. She weighed five thousand eight hundred twelve pounds empty. Maximum speed: three hundred forty-five miles per hour—that's what the book says, but I had her up to five-twenty. Maximum ceiling? Thirty thousand feet—again, the book. I had her up to thirty-six thousand feet. Want to know what she could carry? Two machine guns in the top of the engine cowling plus four mounted on the wings. She carried one six-hundred-pound bomb under each wing. That's a total of sixteen hundred pounds of high explosives. And that's a lot of H.E."

Jackie paused for breath, then continued. "What else can I tell you gentlemen about the P-51 Mustang? Except that whoever dreamed up that name, Mustang, really knew what he or she was talking about, because that's exactly what that airplane was like—she could dance and prance all over the sky and kick up her heels in the hands of an experienced cowboy . . . which is precisely what I was, gentlemen . . . a cowboy—make that cowgirl, but ain't no more. All I am now is—"

She suddenly ran out of breath and fell back on the pillow. The color that had briefly come back to her face left again, leaving Jackie looking as ill as she really was.

"We want to talk to you about one particular Mustang," Will said gently. "A Mustang you crash-landed on a New Mexico desert in '42."

"That happened long ago. I don't want to talk about it." Again she turned her face to the wall.

"Jackie, we've got to talk about it. We've come a long way to get your help. No one else can—" Will stopped and tried a different tack. "We're traveling with the most beautiful P-51 Mustang you've ever seen, fully restored, perfect in every way except one: she's got no engine. We want to find the plane you crash-landed in the desert and see what shape the engine's in. We hope to fix it up and put it in our plane," said Will.

"You guys must be kidding," she said, turning back to face Will and Ben.

"Come to the window and take a look," Ben said. With great difficulty they helped Jackie into her wheelchair along with all of her gear—IV, catheter, monitors—and they wheeled her over to the window. She looked down on *Earth Angel*, gleaming silver in the parking lot. "I never thought I'd see one again," Jackie said as tears from her faded blue eyes ran down the deep creases in her cheeks. "God, she's beautiful."

"How'd you like to see her in the air?" Will asked.

"Do you really think you can get her to fly again?"

"*We*, Jackie. *We* can get her in the air. Ben and I are a couple of pretty good mechanics, but we can't do it without you."

"How can I help? Look at me."

"By telling us where you crash-landed. Where your old P-51 is buried. So we can put your plane's engine into *Earth Angel*."

"I bent two of the prop blades and tore out the belly of the plane, including the air scoop when I crash-landed. That plane's flying days are over."

"And the engine?" Will asked a little too quickly.

"I didn't look too carefully, but it seemed to me that the engine compartment came through okay."

Will said to her then, "Jackie, if we don't get *Earth Angel* flying, she'll wind up a garish sign on top of a gambling casino in Atlantic City—"

Jackie cringed and interrupted. "Tell me about that."

"It's another long story, and so is the story of the flight plan we're following. Right now we don't have time for any more stories." He eyed the corridor where he expected Nurse Crumley anytime now. "It would be better if you told us where you crash-landed the plane."

"Okay, if that's what you want," Jackie began. And then she told them dreamily, "I picked her up at the factory in Detroit. She had five hours on her—you remember, they all had those five hours spent in ground-testing the engine and the instruments. Part of our job was to put the airframe to the test on the delivery flights. A lot of those planes were slapped together and we lost a lot of gals on those test flights.

"Anyway, my job was to fly that P-51 in two legs from Detroit to San Diego. I had done it dozens of times before. I brought her up to about thirty-four thousand feet so I could run her lean to save fuel, because I knew that some of the other stuff I was going to do later in the flight was really going to burn it up. When I got over Dallas, where I was going to put down for some fuel, I was still at thirty-four thousand and practically right over

Love Field, so I tipped her over and put her into a power dive for about thirty-two thousand feet. I got a little too carried away—went too far and too fast. The airspeed indicator was past the red line— way past. I myself was pulling a lot of g's. When I pulled out, I thought sure the wings were going to fall off—but they didn't. I landed and gassed up. Peed. Took right off again.

"An hour or so later I was over New Mexico, and that's where I started to do my stuff. It was my last chance before San Diego to have a little fun without anybody seeing me and maybe reporting it. I did it all—barrel rolls, double hammerheads, spins—you name it, I did them all and added a few new twists. At one point I took her back up to about twenty-five thousand feet and put her into a spin. God how I loved to spin them out. In those days I'd rather spin than—well, anyway, after six or seven spins that bled off a lot of altitude, I crossed the controls and gave her right aileron and opposite rudder to get her out of the spin.

"The instant I stepped on the left rudder pedal, I heard something crack and knew what it was. It was the sound of the horizontal elevator cable snapping. I immediately felt it in the controls. They went dead, and I knew that in the next eighty or ninety seconds I would be dead too. I was in a spin in a plane I couldn't control. I tried everything, but nothing worked.

"The plane was falling at an incredible rate of speed. I gave up trying; I knew there was nothing I could do. Don't ask me how it happened—you know you're not supposed to get out of a spin without an elevator—but at fifteen hundred feet she pulled out of it by herself and leveled off.

"Then I saw it. Directly in front of me was a mountain. . . . I pulled the power—one old aeronautical engineer told me that God saved me that day for something else—I knew I had just one shot at a landing, so I took it and set it down, wheels up, on the smooth-as-glass hot desert sand. Desert sand is different from beach sand, and I was able to roll out for a few hundred feet. She was damaged, like I said, but I wasn't—and I don't think her engine was, either.

"I came to a stop, and not more than fifty yards ahead of me was that mountain—I later learned it's called Apache Mountain.

"If I told the truth about what happened, I would have been court-martialed and thrown out. I never would have flown again. So I said I developed engine trouble and had to put her down in a sandstorm. Just in case they decided to try to find her and dig her up, I told them I landed on the leeward side of the mountain, when in fact, I had landed on the windward side. I also told them that within fifteen minutes of landing, the plane had been completely covered over by the sandstorm.

"The truth is I spent the next eight hours burying her in the sand with my bare hands. As far as I know, they never tried very hard to find her. There was a war going on and everyone had more important things to do. In peacetime there would have been a hundred men and all kinds of equipment out there looking."

"A perfectly good airplane buried alive," Will heard himself say and was immediately sorry he had.

"Go ahead, rub it in! Don't you think I've had to live with that? So, now you know what kind of a lady you're dealing with."

"Those were the actions of a kid . . . a wild kid," said Ben.

"Two days after the crash I walked out of the desert, dehydrated and sunburned. I hitched a ride and told my story—my lie. A little while later I got my orders to ferry a squadron of B-17s to Okinawa. I tried to put the buried P-51 at the foot of Apache

Mountain out of my mind, but I couldn't. Even after all these years, I think about that buried plane a lot . . . a whole lot. Lately I've been thinking more about her . . . and now you guys show up when I'm like this . . . close to. . . . Funny coincidence."

"It might not be a coincidence," said Ben. He looked at Will. "Will and I have been discoverin' new things about coincidences." He told Jackie briefly about how he and Will had met, about Skyros Rexus and the worn piece of paper that was their flight plan with the VA 1040 notation on it. "You don't always get to understand. Doin' it's the main thing, I think," Ben finished.

"Maybe my plane's engine *is* meant to make *Earth Angel* fly again," Jackie mused. "I probably could find her again. . . ."

"We *are* going to find that plane without being caught by Rexus, dig her up, see if we can get her engine going, and then put it into *Earth Angel*," Will said with a determination that surprised even him. "If that doesn't work, I'd just as soon bury *Earth Angel* right there, next to one of her sisters, rather than see her desecrated."

Ben noticed that Will's eyes glistened above his firmly set jawline. "I'll bet if you do find her, there's a good chance the engine will be okay," Ben said, anxious to change the subject. "It's bone dry, and the hot sand is a great insulator—just look at the pyramids and what they've found inside them, perfectly preserved."

"The trick is to find her," countered Jackie. "How do we know what's there now? Fifty-five years later—there might be a McDonald's hamburger joint on top of her or an Indian gambling casino. It'll be almost impossible to find her, but it would be absolutely impossible to find her without me. I have to go with you guys."

"You can't do that, Jackie," Will said. "You're all hooked up. We're just going to have to find it by ourselves. We need you to draw a map as detailed as you can make it."

"What do I need to stay here for? Sure, I could draw you a map and probably get you to within five or ten square miles of where I put her down. But if I go along with you, I bet I can pinpoint an area the size of a football field. Then with a metal detector, we could look for her and have a decent chance of finding her. I'm feeling better already, at just the thought of getting out of here."

"Will's right. You're in no condition to leave here." But as Ben spoke these words, he had to admit that there was more color in her face than when they'd arrived. Still, he persisted. "Besides, it's a long trip—almost two thousand miles from here—and it's wild out there on those roads when you're drivin' a P-51. . . ." But the more he talked, the more he began to think that perhaps it wasn't such a crazy idea.

He looked at Will and could tell that Will was thinking the same thing.

"Look at those numbers on my heart monitor over there," Jackie argued. "My pulse has gone up twenty beats a minute since I saw that plane of yours parked out there. That's the best thing that's happened to me in months! I don't want to sit here and watch my numbers go down and my lines get flatter and flatter."

Ben glanced at the monitor and noticed that right over it was a clipboard with Jackie's full name, address, blood type, and other medical data. What caught his eye was the number written in the space marked SERVICE SERIAL NUMBER: 12457941. It was the number following 712, after VA 1040 on the list in his pocket. He thought back to that first night in Rockport, how those numbers had puzzled both him and Will. He was about to point out the serial number to Will when Jackie continued her plea.

"Please, guys, I'm asking you to do this for me." Determination gave strength to her tone as she finished with "Don't leave me here."

Will and Ben looked at Jackie and then at each other. Before they could respond Jackie sat up, pulled out her IV, pulled the monitor sensors off her chest, and with both hands under the sheet, grimaced as she yanked out the Foley catheter.

"Okay, so now I'm not hooked up anymore," she said. "Let's go."

At that moment Lieutenant Crumley came into the room. "Time to say good-bye, gentlemen. The patient needs her rest and—" Then she saw what Jackie had just done.

Before she could object, Jackie said, "My friends are just leaving, and so am I." She struggled to her feet and handed the nurse the IV bag with its needle and stand, and the catheter.

"Miss Larson, you can't go anywhere! You're a very sick woman. What will I tell your doctor?"

"Tell him . . . tell him I'm on my way to give a lady a heart transplant!"

CHAPTER NINE

On the Road Again

The next day was one of those picture-perfect days in central Illinois, and *Earth Angel* and her crew streaked across the state averaging fifty miles an hour. The sun and the fresh air and perhaps the fact that she was behind the controls of an airplane again, even one that was ground-bound, brought about a near-miraculous change in Jackie Larson. In just twelve hours she looked younger and healthier and appeared to be in no pain. *Earth Angel* continued its westward course, mostly on four-lane highways and always in the slow lane, annoying some drivers, fascinating others.

They had just gone through Wheaton, Illinois, on Route 88, when Will said, "We've got a long way to go, and we're going to need some money. I've got about thirty dollars left and my Sears charge and a couple of gasoline credit cards. We're going to have to economize—quit stopping at fast-food places, maybe eat more C rations, do whatever we can to stretch our cash."

"I got eleven bucks," said Ben. "We better rob the first bank we see. . . . We've got the perfect get-away car!"

"Jeez, you haven't got fifty bucks between you, and we've got about fifteen hundred miles to go," Jackie said smugly.

"We'll make it," Will said. "We should be okay if we watch expenses."

"Lucky for you guys that you met up with the quote, estate of Jacqueline Larson, unquote. And lucky for you guys, too, that the old gal put away a few bucks for her old age. And lucky for you guys again that she's not going to need it in her older age. Pull off the road at the next town, and I'll get us enough to get us where we're going."

Earth Angel pulled into the parking lot of the Rock Island, Illinois, branch of First Chicago. Jackie climbed out of the cockpit, leaving the motor running, took out her ATM card, punched in some numbers, and came back with a wad of bills, saying, "Always said I'd like to spend my last buck on my last day. Maybe I'll get my wish."

The traffic in Peoria was the worst they'd encountered anywhere. *Earth Angel* was wide and she was slow. She was also a spectacle, with Ben and Jackie hanging on to whatever they could find to hang on to, while Will, in the cockpit, threaded through the downtown traffic.

Will was worried. "We've got to get out of this traffic. If we get rear-ended, she'll never fly. Besides, I have a feeling Sky King and Woody are out looking for us by now, so we'd better keep out of sight as much as possible. I've looked at the map and we can take some back roads and eventually get back on our flight-plan highways."

"It's going to take us a lot longer if we take the back roads," said Ben, "but we stand a better chance of getting there in one piece, I guess."

"I just want to remind you guys that I don't have all the time in the world," said Jackie. "I think we better figure on driving day and night with one of us driving, one of us on the traffic-side wing to stand watch. That way one of us can catch a few hours' sleep."

And for the next twenty-four hours, that was what they did. They drove day and night—two hours on, two off. Jackie took her turns and never missed a watch. Her health seemed to improve with each hour and with each mile.

CHAPTER TEN

The Bridge

It happened on their third day after leaving Chicago, *Earth Angel*'s eighth day on the road. A few minutes before midnight Ben glanced down at his wristwatch. He thought about how good it would feel when Will, who was on wing watch and scheduled to drive the midnight-to-two shift, took over. Jackie was asleep in the cramped space behind the second seat in the cockpit. Earlier in the evening, she'd insisted that she wanted to drive the two-to-four shift, but Ben and Will had already made up their minds that if she was still sleeping, they would not wake her, and Ben would work that shift. Besides, both Ben and Will had noticed that Jackie was better in daylight, although neither said anything to Jackie or to each other about that. Suddenly *Earth Angel*'s high beam on the port side picked up a road sign that read:

NARROW BRIDGE—ONE LANE

"How narrow?" Ben wondered under his breath as he pulled back on the throttle and gently applied the brakes.

Twenty seconds later, there it was in front of him—a covered bridge—narrow and low. He jammed on the brakes and brought the plane to a screeching stop about eighteen inches from the entrance to the bridge and a sign that read:

OVERHEAD CLEARANCE 10 FEET
WIDTH 12 FEET.

They were so close to the narrow entrance that Ben was afraid to take his foot off the brake pedals even after he pulled up on the parking brake, fearing that the plane would roll just the few inches it would take to plow it into the sides of the bridge.

In fractions-of-an-inch increments, he carefully took his foot off the brakes, ready to jump back on them in an instant if the plane rolled. The parking brakes held.

The sudden stop jarred Jackie awake, and the three quickly climbed down from *Earth Angel*.

"Another few feet, and we would have been rocket ship *Earth Angel*—no wings, just body!" said Ben.

Jackie looked up at the sign on the side of the bridge that gave its height and width measurements and quickly calculated. "Over nineteen feet too narrow and almost two feet too low. It would have sheared off our wings and part of our tail section, that's for sure."

"It looks like all we can do now is turn around, get back on the highway, and take our chances with the traffic. At least we won't run into any of this kind of stuff," Ben said.

"That means going back to approximately where we were at noon today—about ninety miles," said Jackie.

"That's right, but we can't go ahead," said Ben.

"And we can't go around it," said Jackie. "And we certainly can't go sideways. Anybody got any ideas?"

Will ignored the question and instead took out his pencil and pad and began to make some quick calculations. He threw a handful of dry grass into the wind and went back to his calculations. Finally, he looked up at Ben and Jackie and said, "*Earth Angel* is still an airplane, and you're still a pilot,

Jackie. We're going to fly her over this bridge."

"You ain't going soft in the head, are you, Will?" she said. "This old gal of yours hasn't been three inches off the ground in fifty years. She only has a souped-up car engine, you know that. Buicks don't fly. How are you going to get her in the air?"

"I'm not. You are, Jackie. The P-51 lifts off at eighty miles an hour in about eighteen-hundred feet—that's with full tanks, guns on the wings, ten thousand rounds of fifty-caliber ammo, and two five-hundred-pound bombs. We're light by those standards. No doubt that we're short on horse-power, but we ought to be able to lift her off in a third of that distance, say six hundred to seven hundred feet, with a running start. Ben and I'll get out, for starters.

"Buicks can back up, don't forget. You need to back her up about a thousand feet. Rev her up. Give her full bore.

"When you get her up to between sixty-five and sixty-eight miles per hour, pull back on the stick gently and she should lift off. No reason why she wouldn't.

"She should clear the bridge with something like ten or twelve feet to spare—that is, if the wind doesn't shift or pick up. Once over, you should still have enough lift to set her down on the road on the other side."

"Ten or twelve feet to spare. What if—" Jackie said.

Ignoring her objection, Will said, "We'll meet you on the other side. She can do it. You can do it too, Jackie."

"But I haven't been at the controls of an airplane in over twenty years—"

Will either didn't hear Jackie's last comment—or pretended he didn't hear it—as he walked up to *Earth Angel* and put one hand on her cowling and rested the other on the spinner of her prop. Head down, he began speaking softly to *Earth Angel*. Jackie and Ben couldn't hear what he was saying, but there was no doubt that he was actually talking to her.

Ben reminded himself that people spoke to animals all the time, and that animals listened and often seemed to understand. Sometimes—mostly in movies or in novels—it worked with inanimate objects, too. Seeing Will and *Earth Angel* at that moment, Ben Mapes and Jackie Larson sensed that there was something out of the ordinary happening here—something similar to what Ben had seen happen in the blue light of the barn and to what

Jackie had felt happen when her body had so quickly recovered enough strength to join *Earth Angel*'s mission, whatever that mission was.

It seemed clear to them that somehow the plane was understanding what Will was asking of her. Ben and Jackie felt this through some kind of sixth or seventh sense. But the question was, could the plane do it? Would the laws of physics allow her to?

After a minute or two Will said, "She's ready. Climb in and take her back, Jackie. Ben and I will cross the bridge and set up some road flares on the other side."

Jackie climbed up on the wing and back into the cockpit. She started the old Buick engine, threw the supercharger switch, and put the Dynaflo transmission in reverse. *Earth Angel* went backward approximately a thousand feet—maybe a little more. Jackie set the brakes and revved up the engine. With the tachometer approaching the red-line area, Jackie released the brakes. *Earth Angel* leaped forward and started her roll down the yellow line of the two-lane road. The airspeed indicator quickly got up to 30, 40, 50, 55, 56, 57, 58, 59, 60—and stayed at 60. They were two hundred feet from the bridge.

Just as Jackie thought it would never budge beyond 60, the needle literally jumped from 60 to 80. At that moment *Earth Angel*'s wheels left the ground for the first time in fifty years. The bridge was now less than fifty yards in front—half a football field away. Suddenly, the plane lunged upward, unsteady and wobbly, but upward nonetheless. *Earth Angel*'s wing lights briefly picked up the green-copper rooster weather vane on the roof of the bridge and the darkness beyond. *Earth Angel* struggled for altitude against the familiar force of gravity that was trying to pull her down. Just when she thought she'd succeeded, Jackie heard a loud thud from under the plane. She had cleared the bridge . . . but not the rooster.

Will and Ben had ducked instinctively as the plane passed over their heads at an altitude of no more than twenty-five feet. In an instant, it was all over. Jackie set *Earth Angel* down on the road on the other side of the bridge between the flares and brought the plane to a full stop. Jackie shut off the engine and slumped down in her seat, motionless in the red glow of the road flares.

Will and Ben ran up to her, and before Ben climbed on the wing to get to Jackie in the cockpit, he noticed that the rooster weather vane was snarled and tangled in *Earth Angel's* landing gear. An easy repair for *Earth Angel*, he thought, but what about Jackie? Was she all right? Was it too much for her heart to take?

After a moment or two in the cockpit Jackie slowly moved and looked around at the smiling faces of her comrades.

"She's still an airplane," Jackie said.

"She sure is, and you're still quite a pilot," said Will.

"I guess I am . . . I guess I am," she said, her voice husky from exhaustion.

CHAPTER ELEVEN

And God Told Noah . . .

The covered bridge had taken its toll. It was a victory, but like all victories it came at a price. It proved that *Earth Angel* could still fly and that Jackie could fly her and that Will hadn't lost either his confidence or his willingness to take a risk—risking even *Earth Angel*. But it left the three of them exhausted. Even *Earth Angel* looked . . . well, she looked different somehow.

They decided to pull off the road for the night, and it was a good thing they did, because minutes later the rain came—and lots of it. It rained just as hard as it had the night they'd left Rockport, and the three of them huddled together around a small campfire they built under the shelter of one wing.

Coffee never tasted as good as it did that night. "It must have been a night like this when God whispered into Noah's ear that he should build an ark," said Ben, looking up at the water pouring off the trailing edge of the wing.

"I used to love that Bible story when I was a kid," said Jackie. "It could be true, you know. Geologists say there was a great flood that covered the earth and actually formed the Dead Sea. One of our old astronauts—I forget which one—thinks there really was an ark, and he took a couple of expeditions up Mount Arafat to look for it."

"You mean Ararat, not Arafat," said Ben.

"Oh, that's right. Arafat's the PLO guy with the scraggly beard and the designer dish towel on his head," said Jackie.

Ben was about to tell her it was called a kaffiyeh when Will, who had been gazing off into space and deep in his own thoughts, suddenly sat up straight and asked, "What did you just say?"

"I said Arafat isn't the mountain—"

"No. Before that."

"We were talkin' about God whisperin' in Noah's ear and tellin' him to build an ark."

"That's it!" said Will, jumping to his feet and ignoring the fact that he was out from under the protection of the wing and getting soaked. "That's what we have to do. We have to build an ark—a raft, in our case—and float *Earth Angel* as close to Texas as we can get."

"Will, we're in the dead center of the country," said Jackie. "Texas is fifteen-hundred miles overland. The nearest body of water is . . . "

"Is the Mississippi River," said Will. "We are seventy-five, maybe a hundred, miles away from the northernmost tributaries of the Mississippi River. We could build a raft, float her down the Mississippi and into the Gulf of Mexico, and pull in somewhere in Texas. Then we'd be able to drive her along those long, straight, wide Texas highways . . . right into New Mexico."

Without waiting for a response, Will climbed up on the wing and reached into the cockpit to get the old Esso road map that had been their chart, just as the scrap of yellowed paper had been their "flight plan." Ducking back under the wing and wiping the water from his face, he said, "Look here. We're about eighty miles south of Prairie du Chien, Wisconsin. There was a guy in my outfit from around there, and I remember him telling me about a logging operation there. He said the largest cargo-carrying log raft ever to go down the

Mississippi was built there. It was as wide as a football field and extended over a quarter of a mile.

"As soon as this weather lets up, I say we should head for Prairie du Chien and build a raft."

"What about our flight plan?" said Ben. "What does it say we should do between here and Texas?" He reached into his wallet and took out the scrap of paper and with the other hand spread out the road map. "It's here! Zero-six-zero—Route 60—leads into Prairie du Chien, and right under zero-six-zero is 'MR,' which I always thought stood for mister. But it could stand for Mississippi River.

"We can take the Mississippi River south to New Orleans, and hug the Louisiana coast to Port Arthur or Galveston, dock, and head west."

As the three looked at each other, ready to accept the new plan, it stopped raining—suddenly and completely. And, as on the night they'd left Rockport, the sky cleared and the stars came out.

Will and Ben and Jackie came out from under the wing and looked up at the stars, grateful that, for the first time since they'd decided to journey together, they were sure of the route they were meant to take to Apache Mountain. It didn't matter what might happen along the way or when they got there. What mattered was the fact that the numbers on the tattered piece of once-white paper did indeed make sense. And that the three of them were meant to follow that "flight plan" together.

It was a night that all of them would remember for the rest of their lives.

CHAPTER TWELVE

It's an Aircraft Carrier!

The men who worked at the Prairie du Chien Logging Company stopped what they were doing when *Earth Angel*, with Jackie in the cockpit and Ben and Will standing on the wings, pulled into their parking lot. The sawmill operation stopped sawing. The forklift trucks stopped lifting. The clerks put down their pencils and turned away from their computers. And Johnnie Fox, a Sioux and the owner of the company, stood in the doorway of his office shaking his head in disbelief. A few minutes later the crew of *Earth Angel* was inside Johnnie Fox's office.

"That's our story, Mr. Fox. Can you help us?" asked Will after he explained why they'd come.

"We have some money, so we're not asking for charity. We need you and your men to build us a raft. Any day now, Rexus will decide to look for us, if he hasn't started already. One Chicago radio station ran a report on Jackie here walking out of the VA Hospital with us. Then there was another news report on a near miss we had with a semi a couple of days ago, so you see we need the raft right away—today if possible, tomorrow at the latest."

Johnnie Fox thought for a moment, stroked his chin, and said gravely, "Your experience with the Mississippi River is limited to what you read as children in *Huckleberry Finn*—a wonderful adventure story, very romantic, too—but you've got to remember it's fiction. The fact is, the Mississippi River can be very dangerous, even treacherous. Sometimes it's like an ocean, sometimes like a lake. In some places it's miles wide; in others you can practically touch both shores. Sometimes it's swift; sometimes it's dead calm. You have to navigate down the river, you can't just float. And you have to learn its backwaters.

"To sail the Mississippi, you need three things—you need to be able to steer, you need power, and you need brakes. Without those things, you won't get ten miles before you bottom out or hit the shore or crash into other river traffic or they ram you.

"The Mississippi is a superhighway running right through the middle of the country from north to south, carrying billions of tons of cargo every day. It's a dangerous place if you don't know what you're doing."

"We're pilots, John, and on the way here I worked on figuring out the steering, braking, and power our plane can contribute," said Will, taking out his small pad. "We'll use the plane to operate the raft. *Earth Angel* has a rudder and ailerons to catch the wind; that will steer the raft. Her wings and prop can propel the raft forward, and her wing flaps will brake when we need to slow down."

"A good start, but you'll need more of those things—especially the steering and braking—than your airplane can provide . . . much more." Johnnie Fox got up from his desk and walked outside. Arms folded across his chest, he gazed out at the river as if looking to it for answers. An hour passed like that. Johnnie Fox seemed to be barely breathing.

Then he suddenly came back to life, turned to the crew of *Earth Angel*, and said, "You'll have your raft and everything it needs to get you to where you're going. . . . We'll work all night, and you'll have it tomorrow."

Will, Ben, and Jackie watched, and helped however they could. They helped saw the timbers that would make up the deck of their raft; they watched as they were lashed together with heavy rope and metal cleats; they smiled as the little shanty, which would be their outhouse and shower, was erected on it.

A little more than twenty-four hours later, the finishing touches of red and green port and starboard lights, and their raft was finished. *Earth Angel* was carefully rolled onto the raft and lashed to the deck. Then, with the help of two forklift trucks—one pushing and the other pulling—and twelve strong men pulling on ropes tied to the raft, the raft came to the bank of the river. With one giant effort they pushed her down the river access and into the Mississippi River. The raft began to sink. It was sinking slowly—by inches—but it was sinking. The deck sank three feet below the surface and the brown, still water covered *Earth Angel*'s wheels. From the bank of the river, it looked as if the plane were floating on its wings. Will, Ben, and Jackie couldn't believe what they were seeing. Their hearts were sinking with the raft. They were powerless to do anything. Had they come all this way only to see *Earth Angel* sink to a muddy, watery grave?

Suddenly the raft began to rise up, and soon the deck appeared just below the surface of the water. Seconds later the entire deck was floating well above the water.

"That always happens with a new raft," said Johnnie matter-of-factly. "It takes a few minutes for it to adjust to the water and float. I should have told you to expect it."

One by one Ben, Will, and Jackie said their thanks and good-byes to the men who had worked so hard to make this moment happen. Finally, it was Will's turn to say good-bye to Johnnie Fox.

"John, you don't know what this means to us. . . . We haven't talked about money. If we don't have enough on us, we'll send it to you. I promise we will." Will reached for his wallet.

"This one's on us," said Johnnie Fox simply. "You have a long way to go and the spirits tell me that those who are going to pursue you are gathering their forces and will soon be upon you. You should leave now."

The three jumped on the raft and untied it, and they began to drift downriver.

Ten minutes later they had their first of many encounters on the Mississippi River. A barge worker sailing upriver cupped his hands to his mouth and yelled, "What is it?"

Jackie, cupping her hands, shouted in return, "Don't you know an aircraft carrier when you see one, sailor?"

CHAPTER THIRTEEN

Down the Mississippi

For the next four days, in all kinds of weather and navigating all kinds of currents amid all kinds of river traffic, the raft floated south on the Mississippi River. Each day brought a new challenge and sometimes even an adventure. They quickly learned that everything Johnnie Fox had told them about this mightiest of all the rivers in the world was true. There were the backwaters to learn. Sometimes the river was like a lake, other times like an ocean. In some places the river was ten miles wide, and in others it was so narrow they had to navigate carefully to keep from running aground.

On the second day, a fog engulfed them. It was

so thick they couldn't see as far as the wing tips. A short time later they had a very near miss with a side-wheeler riverboat, the *Samuel L. Clemens*, whose powerful diesel turbines could have easily chewed up their raft in a single revolution of her sixty-foot wheel.

The next day, during a violent electrical storm, one of *Angel's* wheel lashes broke loose and the chock washed overboard, causing the other lash to snap seconds later. *Earth Angel* started to slide into the muddy waters of the Mississippi.

The three of them grabbed on to *Earth Angel*—Jackie to the tail section, despite her frailty, Will and Ben to the wheels—and pulled with all their might as though each were years younger. Somehow they hefted her 5,812 pounds back onto the deck without tipping the raft over. They all knew, as they pulled her to safety and lashed her back to the deck, that they weren't pulling that weight up alone—they could feel an invisible hand tugging with them. They did not understand it and they didn't attempt to. They were getting used to being thankful for things they didn't understand.

On the fourth day the raft got caught in rapids. Ben was swept overboard and nearly drowned.

A few hours later the raft and *Earth Angel* were

nearly dashed to pieces against the rocky shore. But again they were helped. And again they accepted it. They pressed on, always alert to the dangers at almost every bend in this mighty and unpredictable river.

On the fifth day they got a lift. They were able to hitch a ride behind a thirty-five-barge caravan towed by the riverboat *Alice B. Hooker*. That free ride, as Ben called it, lasted for almost a hundred miles, and gave them a measure of security and the rest they needed. As they gave their thanks to the skipper of the *Alice B.* and watched her steam out of sight, they wondered what else awaited them on this dangerous but magnificent river, which cut through the center of the country they all loved and had risked their lives to defend.

"According to my calculations, if the current holds steady, we're going to be passing St. Louis about four or five o'clock tomorrow afternoon. Might be a good chance for you to call your husband, Jackie," Will said. "Maybe even see him for an hour or so."

"He's not my husband anymore; he's somebody else's husband. Besides, I don't want him to see me like this—sick. I don't want to scare him. Sometimes I catch a look at myself, in that mirror in our little shanty here, and I scare myself."

"A little pale, maybe, but you don't look so bad, considerin'—" said Ben, stopping in midsentence. "You look a lot better than you did in that hospital bed, that's for sure. We could even buff you up a bit more if you were goin' out on a date."

"It's the right thing to do, Jackie," said Will. "You may not get another chance to see him for a long time."

"I don't have a long time," Jackie grumbled. "I'll think about it."

The next day Will and Ben were handling the navigating and piloting and Jackie was sitting on the deck looking off into space, deep in her thoughts. The raft passed a sign on the bank that read SEVEN MILES TO ST. LOUIS. Will and Ben saw it, and they were sure that Jackie did, too. A short time later Saarinen's arch came into view. Another sign told them it was five miles to St. Louis. Then three miles. Two miles, and then the tall buildings and the brown haze of the city loomed ahead. Finally, they passed a large colorful sign that said, ENTERING ST. LOUIS, GATEWAY TO THE WEST, and they saw the skyline of the city around the next bend.

Jackie jumped to her feet. "Hard to starboard and make ready to dock," she said in a loud, strong voice.

CHAPTER FOURTEEN

One More Ride

Jackie arrived early at the Gateway to the West Amusement Park—pilots are almost always early. She was standing in front of one of the oldest and most beautiful carousels in America, anxiously looking out at the crowd, when Don came up from behind and gently tapped her on the shoulder.

"Shall we try for the brass ring?" he said. For the first two or perhaps three minutes there were no words, just their long embrace.

"I love you, and I always will, Jackie," he said.

"I love you, too, and always will. I've missed you, Don," said Jackie, her voice choked with emotion. Then she cleared her throat and looked around.

"I can't believe it's still here," she said. "Same horses. Same music. Same kind of night. And you just as handsome now as you were then . . . even more so."

"I come here a lot. Lots of good memories. I'm married to a wonderful woman, but my love for you, Jackie, will always be there in its own special place in my heart. I like coming here. It makes me feel close to you."

"That's nice of you to say after all—"

He interrupted her. "You know I wanted to come up to see you in the hospital in Chicago. I spoke to the doctors and they said it would be okay, but they said you didn't want to see me."

"I did want to see you, but I didn't want you to see me like this . . . like I am now. Besides," she said a little too airily, "I figured I'd be passing through St. Louis someday soon. You know me . . . I get around."

"How *are* you, Jackie?" he asked, looking into her eyes, searching for a real answer.

"Me?" she asked, trying to sound unconcerned. "I'm doing okay . . . a lot better than I was a week ago. I'm traveling with a couple of wonderful guys. You won't believe it, but we've got a beautiful old P-51 on a log raft, and we're going down the river all the way to the Gulf and then into Texas; and from there, we'll make our way across to western New Mexico. You should see this old lady. Her name is *Earth Angel* . . . and she's beautiful."

"She couldn't be more beautiful than you are, Jackie."

"Oh, Don," she said. "I'm so sorry—"

"I'm happy you're back doing something you love. I'm happy it involves an airplane. I'm glad it's a P-51. And now that you're back flying, you'll need these." Don reached into his pocket and pinned Jackie's World War II wings on her shirt. "After you left these behind, I carried them with me every day because I knew how much they meant to you. I know flying has always been your first love. But having them with me made me feel close to you. I may not be your first choice, but you were always mine."

"I'm sorry I've been like that."

"Don't be," he said as he put his finger up to her lips to keep her from saying any more. "I knew that when I married you and—"

"If only I could have stuck it out with the airline job, things might have been different for us. I just couldn't take that flight engineer's job, knowing I'd never get a chance to fly, even as copilot. And then having to listen to the this-is-your-captain-speaking routine, apologizing for delays or a few bumps along the way, pointing out Niagara Falls and Disneyland . . . I choked on having to watch some young pilot stand in the cockpit doorway, collar buttoned, tie up, jacket on, spouting his 'thank you for flying with us, folks' line. I just couldn't take it, and they couldn't take me. After that, it was just a whole string of jobs until I hit bottom. At least in Honduras I could be a pilot again. I shortchanged you, Don. I couldn't even be honest with you. There were even other—"

"You have to stop this, Jackie. That's history. Let it go—I have. All I've kept are the good parts, the wonderful parts, the beautiful memories. All that matters is that we are two people who have known each other for a long time, loved each other from the moment we laid eyes on each other right here in this amusement park almost half a century ago. All that matters is that we are here together and that we still love each other. I never once regretted that love, never once in all the years. Now . . . let's hold each other until it's time for you to go." And they did.

CHAPTER FIFTEEN

Wars

Early the next morning *Earth Angel* quietly slipped away from the Missouri shore and back into the Mississippi's mainstream. Will took out the tattered road map and announced, "From here until we meet the Gulf of Mexico the river drops a little with each mile. That means the current will pick up, so we better put the flaps down and be ready to crab her into the wind if we have to slow her down. If we start to pick up too much speed, we might even have to drag the anchor. And pray that the anchor post holds. If it gives way and we lose the anchor, we have a real problem."

"We could float all the way to Honduras," said Ben, smiling.

The current did get stronger, but they managed it easily. Their luck was holding.

From the beginning of this part of the journey, they were struck by the natural beauty of this end of the Mississippi—the trees lining the shore with their heavily leafed limbs, the wilderness, the magnificent antebellum houses along the banks, the cotton fields, the seas of sugar cane, the river shanties on stilts, the swans and cranes and other wildlife, the Spanish moss, and the hundreds of smells and sounds that went with all of those things.

Over the forty-eight hours they spent on this part of the river, they had a chance to think and to renew themselves. They thought about the past, the present, and mostly about what was to come in the days ahead.

As the raft neared Vicksburg, Mississippi, they began to see the crosses and monuments marking where soldiers of both the North and South fought for control of the river's strategic port. They decided to spend the night in Vicksburg. They camped at the base of a hill, and for supper they ate food that they took from cans and cooked over a soft-wood fire.

"I'm goin' to see what's on the other side of that

hill," Ben said after they cleaned their pots and dishes.

Minutes later Ben was looking down on the war cemetery at Vicksburg. Small white markers stood at each grave, an array of Confederate flags mixed in with the Stars and Stripes and the tall trees and the setting sun. The peacefulness of the scene was stunning. So was the vastness of the cemetery. After a few minutes Ben walked back to where Will and Jackie were finishing up the last of the coffee.

"I want to show you somethin' worth seein'."

A few minutes later Will and Jackie stood on the crest of the hill looking down at the cemetery, moved by what they were looking at, just as Ben was.

"I've read about this place," said Will, speaking barely above a whisper, his voice filled with awe. "There are seventeen thousand men, Confederate and Union soldiers, buried here. Think of it: seventeen thousand men. This spot was where some of the fiercest fighting in the Civil War took place. When it was over, those who survived just buried the dead where they fell."

They walked down the hill, and as they passed the rows of gravestones and the stately monuments, Will said, "This was one of the bloodiest battles of the war. Grant was commanding seventy-five thousand soldiers but knew he couldn't capture heavily fortified Vicksburg from the Confederates, so he went sailing past here and went downriver. I forget how many miles, but way past it—fifty or sixty, I think. His troops disembarked there and then doubled back, hoping to attack the Confederates by surprise from the inland side of the city, which was a weaker point. The Union army settled on some high ground and laid a steady siege to Vicksburg. There was no letup for the next four years.

"Then a barricade was set up. Union gunboats and Grant's artillery kept up the pounding. Both the citizens and the soldiers of Vicksburg dug caves in the hills. Eventually, their food supply gave out. They slaughtered their mules and ate them. Then they slaughtered their horses. In the end, they were eating river rats and swamp grass. Somebody wrote—Walt Whitman, I think it was—that the river here ran red with fire and blood. A thousand men were killed in one battle." After a long pause he continued, "Six hundred and twenty thousand killed in those four years. What a waste—what a shameful, stupid, obscene waste."

"I wonder what it was like for them," Jackie said to Will. "I wonder if the Civil War was anything like our war."

"We'll never know," Will replied, "because I don't think the real wars ever get into the history books. A lot of the facts get distorted, first by politics and patriotism and then by nostalgia. That's the way it is with all wars. That's the way it was with what we call 'our' war—World War II. The so-called good war. For the past fifty years that war has been rewritten by governments and romanticized by sentimentalists, the movies, and millions of just plain war stories that get changed and changed again each time they're told. The fact is, there were almost a hundred million people killed in our war. Two-thirds of them were civilians—men, women, and children caught in the crossfire, the bombings, the artillery barrages, and the gas chambers. Then we dropped the bomb, and when it was all over another kind of war began . . . and another, and another, and another."

Will paused and then changed the subject. They all knew that no words would change history—past or future. "We'd better get back and tuck ourselves in for the night. We have a big day ahead of us. With the strong current, we really could sail past New Orleans and too far into the Gulf. Headed for your old haunts in Honduras, just as Ben said the other day."

CHAPTER SIXTEEN

Rodney

The log that Will was keeping—*Earth Angel*'s original log—described the next day as "uneventful; weather clear; current moderate; all systems on *Earth Angel* and the raft performed well." As the sun began to set over the western bank of the river, they dropped anchor and tied up to a pier that, a sign told them, was in Rodney, Mississippi, population 279. A ten-minute walk away, they found a 1950s-style stainless-steel diner with a blinking, blue neon sign spelling out EATS, though half the letters—the T and the S—didn't light up.

"Look!" Ben said, pointing to the sign. "Only the E and the A are lit up: EA—get it? As in *Earth Angel*? A good omen, maybe."

The three of them paused for a moment, no longer embarrassed to believe in a promise of good fortune. Then they entered the diner, which did not look like, or smell like, any God-given oasis. They sat down in an upholstered booth, which, like the others, had several unrepaired cuts in the red vinyl and an accumulation of grime in its bindings. There were a few slow-moving regulars at the counter bent over heavy coffee mugs, some loud townie kids in the next booth, and a thin, consumptive-sounding man at the griddle, sucking deeply on a Camel between bouts with a rattling cough. From time to time he'd lay his cigarette down on the edge of the griddle, next to the hamburgers he was cooking.

Above the counter, just below the Dr Pepper wall clock with its grease-coated glass front, there was a clean, late-model, large-screen television tuned to the CBS Evening News.

The waitress—a slightly overweight, middle-aged, heavily made-up, bleached blonde—shuffled over to the table and, without looking at them, pulled out an order pad from the pocket of her three-day-old apron. Her name tag said CHERYL.

"What can I get for you three?" Cheryl asked, snapping her gum. Coming through in every word was the attitude that she hated her job, and the thing she hated most about it was waiting on strangers . . . particularly northerners.

"What's good?" asked Ben.

"I don't know nothin' about good, Leroy," she said. "I just work here. I never eat here myself, so don't ask me what's good, okay? Just look up at the board or at the greasy old menu in front of you and tell me what you want and I'll tell you if we got any left. That's the way it works here, okay?"

"Isn't she lovely, Leroy?" said Jackie, turning to Ben. "A true belle of the South. So charming. So gentle. And how do you suppose she knew your name was Leroy?"

"How'd you like a fistful of knuckles for an appetizer?" snapped Cheryl, who was determined to get in the last word and spoiling for a fight.

Jackie hadn't had a good fight since that cantina in Tegucigalpa, Honduras, when she'd tussled with three women who ganged up on her and had left them in need of medical attention. She began to slide out of the booth, and Ben moved his body between the two women.

Will hadn't been paying much attention to either the menu or this acidic exchange between Cheryl and whomever wanted to listen to her. He was preoccupied with watching the news on television, when suddenly a set of old pictures of a younger Will and of Ben in Vietnam and of Jackie in her World War II WASP flight suit appeared across the TV screen.

"Listen to this," said Will.

They all looked up at the familiar face of Dan Rather, who was saying:

Finally tonight, on our "Eye on America" segment, a most unusual story. One of those it-could-only-happen-in-America stories. It's about two men, one woman, and an old World War II airplane—an airplane that can't fly—that never will fly.

The central character in this story is Will Wright, named after Wilbur Wright, who, with his brother Orville built and flew the first motorized airplane at Kitty Hawk, North Carolina. Will Wright owns and operates a two-pump gas station and garage in Rockport, Massachusetts—a charming little fishing town and artists' colony on Cape Ann.

At the outbreak of World War II, young Will Wright was accepted into the Army Air Corps' pilot training program and graduated first in his class. Nowadays they call such pilots Top Guns. On graduation day a freak accident cost him an eye, and he never flew a single hour after that.

After the war, he searched for his old plane—a P-51 Mustang that he had named Earth Angel—complete with a picture of Katharine Hepburn, his wartime pinup girl, painted on the cowling. Years later he found the plane, literally hacked it out of the jungle, and restored it to perfect condition except for one thing. It didn't have an engine. And there wasn't one to be had anywhere. After a few years, Will fitted his plane with a 1947 Buick eight-cylinder engine, which had enough power to turn the prop a little and run some of the controls—light up the panel, work the radio, and turn the wheels.

Twelve days ago, Will and a homeless Vietnam vet—a journeyman mechanic named Benjamin Mapes, drove off in the middle of the night in the plane. They headed west. Along the way they stopped at the veterans hospital in Chicago to pick up a third member of the crew, Jackie Larson, also a pilot and a World War II veteran. Jackie is Jacqueline Larson, the only woman combat pilot in that war, although she was never authorized and never recognized officially. She flew with General Claire Chennault's famed Flying Tigers, but when she was discovered by Washington to be a woman, she had to finish out the war as a WASP, ferrying planes to the front, testing them, and, I'm told, even pulling targets for practicing anti-aircraft gunners . . . a dangerous occupation. CBS News has learned that Jackie is now terminally ill.

A week ago she pulled out the life-supporting IV and catheter she was tethered to, and the three piled into Earth Angel *with its souped-up Buick engine and headed west on the interstate. There have been many reported sightings—mostly by children, and oddly enough, none by law enforcement officers. When last seen two days ago, the three were floating down the Mississippi River on a log raft holding them and* Earth Angel. *Their ultimate destination is not known.*

At this point, you are probably smiling and thinking what a charming adventure these three are having in their senior years. Well, according to reliable sources, CBS has learned that the three are actually fleeing from the billionaire playboy and airline, shipping, and international gambling tycoon, Skyros Rexus, known to most as Sky King. It seems that a few years ago Will Wright put up the P-51 as collateral on a second mortgage on his business. With business bad, Will Wright fell behind on the loan payments, so the bank looked for a buyer of that collateral and found one in Sky King.

King plans to hoist the rare old plane to the top of his new Atlantic City casino, The Sky's the Limit, *so named because the casino will take any size bet. CBS*

News has also learned that Skyros Rexus has a small army—and now a navy—out looking for the plane at this very moment. They are using helicopters and speedboats in an attempt to find Earth Angel. *Rexus, a large contributor to both the Republican and Democratic parties, has considerable clout with the Administration, and reportedly has talked the government into joining in the search. They're using Coast Guard boats and helicopters to search a hundred-fifty-square-mile area from the Gulf of Mexico as far north as Vicksburg, Mississippi, where they were last seen. The Pentagon confirmed to CBS News tonight that the Coast Guard has orders to stop the raft, board her, take the three into custody, and tow the raft to the nearest port.*

A sad sidelight to this story: Will Wright's child, First Lieutenant Casey Wright, was also a pilot, and in 1968 he was killed in action over Vietnam while flying his Phantom jet.

Mrs. Wright, who lives in Erie, Pennsylvania, says she has not been in touch with her husband since last Christmas. She expressed concern for his safety.

A footnote: We caught up with Miss Hepburn today at her Fenwick, Connecticut, home, and asked her what she thought of all this. She replied with her characteristic candor, clarity, and spunk.

Katharine Hepburn's face filled the TV screen as her words were broadcast.

"I think it is simply wonderful what these three are doing. It's so romantic. It's so American. Three comrades-in-arms floating down the Mississippi on a raft with a plane they obviously love, dodging that awful man and his army of . . . goons. Delightful! A quest: Exciting. I wish I could be on that raft with them. I'm all for them. The whole country should be cheering them on. I say help them, or at least have the courtesy to get out of their way. As for the Pentagon, they should mind their own damn business."

The picture returned to Dan Rather as he did the story's closeout:

Here at CBS News we try to be evenhanded in bringing you the news and try to stay away from editorial comments. But tonight we are going to break with that tradition, because I must say that this reporter shares Miss Hepburn's view.

We'll keep you updated on this unusual story in the days ahead. That's it for all of us here at CBS News. Dan Rather reporting. See you back here tomorrow. Good night.

"Atta girl, Kate!" said Ben, jumping to his feet and punching the air.

"Even my doctors never told me I'm terminal. How do you like that? I'm officially told I'm dying by Dan Rather on national TV," Jackie said, laughing.

None of the three noticed that the two deep furrows above the bridge of the waitress's nose seemed to have disappeared, and with them the perpetual frown on her face. Nor did they also notice that Cheryl was biting her lower lip to hold back the tears that welled in her eyes. She seemed, now, younger, more full of life—almost beautiful—as she once had been.

But they all knew that things had suddenly turned serious for them. "'Small army . . . boats . . . helicopters . . . tow her to the nearest port.' We've got to get back to the ship," said Ben.

"If they catch us, it's all over, and God knows what will happen to *Earth Angel*," Will said.

"And they've got a good shot at catchin' us, Will. You know that. It's tough to hide a plane on that river. They have radar and all sorts of trackin' devices. Somewhere between here and where we're goin', they're goin' to spot us," Ben said.

"We're going to have to travel at night," said Will. "Lucky there's a full moon and clear skies forecast for the next few nights. If we stay close to the banks of the river and hide ourselves in out-of-the-way spots during the day, we'll make it."

"They ain't gonna catch y'all, don't worry none about that," said Cheryl, taking them all by surprise. Her voice, too, had become softer and friendlier. "They ain't gonna catch y'all because you are all good people, and God looks out for the good people. Y'all are in the right and they ain't, so don't worry about nothin'. And don't go runnin' off until you get your eats, which Buford over there is fixin'. And while y'all are eatin', Buford and I will be packin' up some soup and sandwiches and some cold chicken that should last you a few days. We might even be able to find a few homemade pies and throw them in for good measure. And don't embarrass yourselves by tryin' to pay with your Yankee money. Your money ain't no good at the Rodney Diner. Ain't that right, Buford?"

"That's right, Cheryl," Buford croaked, which was all the lump in his throat allowed him to say as he turned back to his griddle.

Will, Ben, and Jackie could not speak, but their eyes met Cheryl's and said it all.

An hour and a half later the three piled into the flatbed of Buford's pickup, which was loaded with food and held Cheryl in the front seat.

Cheryl was stunned at her first sight of *Earth*

Angel. "She's beautiful—just beautiful! Somethin' like this is worth riskin' it all, which is what y'all are doin'," she said.

With the food loaded onto the raft, they were ready to shove off. "Cheryl, we don't know how to thank you and Buford," said Jackie as she put her arms around the waitress and gently kissed her cheek. Will followed.

Ben hesitated.

"I want to apologize to you, Ben, for the 'Leroy' stuff," she said.

Then she turned to the others and said, "I learned somethin' tonight. Here I've been stuck on how I ended up back here in Rodney when dancin' in New Orleans didn't land me in Vegas like I planned. Been blamin' that guy who promised and didn't come through with a job. But all this time I haven't even been noticin' anybody around here. How good most of 'em are. And how you gotta stand up to the bad guys. Thanks for wakin' me up." She brushed away tears.

"You're a good lady, Cheryl. You got a lotta heart . . . and soul. Take it from someone who knows somethin' about soul," said Ben, his eyes glistening in the moonlight. It was the first time Will had seen a tear roll down Ben's cheek. It did not leave a white streak.

For the next two days they traveled at night and hid during the day. They got good at navigating at night—they had to. The dark made the other boat traffic, the half-submerged islands, and the rapids even more dangerous. All they had were flashlights, but they managed to make progress downriver without being seen.

Twice they came close to being discovered. The first time, four very tough-looking guys in a fast powerboat bearing the name Sky King Enterprises came within twenty feet of the raft. Two of them appeared to be looking directly at the raft, but their expressionless faces told the crew of *Earth Angel* that they were not seeing anything. It was as if *Earth Angel* were suddenly invisible.

"They were lookin' right at us. How could they have missed us?" said Ben.

No one had an answer.

The other time they were sure they'd been found, a Coast Guard patrol boat passed not more than fifteen feet across the bow of the raft, and not one of the eight men on deck saw *Earth Angel*. It was as if they were looking right through the raft, *Earth Angel*, and her crew of three.

Yet others on the banks and on the river at night

saw them and waved and gave them a thumbs-up and cheered them on. Will, Ben, and Jackie had no idea how it was that the forces out looking for them did not see them but the well-wishers did. Whatever it was, they were grateful for it.

After three days they drifted past New Orleans and turned left around Grand Isle. They hugged the coast past Houma and threaded their way between Marsh Island and the mainland. Two days later they arrived just outside Galveston on the Gulf of Mexico.

"We'll hide here during the daylight hours," said Will. "And then, as soon as it starts to get dark, we'll roll *Earth Angel* off, sink the raft, and get on Highway 111. We should make San Antonio by daylight, hide her again, and day after tomorrow, with luck, we should be looking at Apache Mountain."

"Sounds easy when you say it fast like that, but there's a lot of miles to cover between here and where we're going. And a lot of wide open spaces with no place to hide," Jackie said.

Will, Ben, and Jackie began breaking off tree branches to camouflage *Earth Angel*. Off in the distance they heard the unmistakable sound of a helicopter. It was getting louder.

CHAPTER SEVENTEEN

Trouble from Above

They saw him the same instant he saw them. Randy Kane, Odessa KOTX-AM Skyway Patrol helicopter pilot and reporter, hovered over the scene for a couple of minutes just to make sure it was them. He dropped down a little lower for a closer look, then picked up his mike and rolled his tongue to shift the wad of Red Man chewing tobacco from the right side of his cheek to the left side because he felt he talked better with it on the left. Like most men, Randy had preferences for left or right when it came to almost everything. He hit the button on his mike.

"KOTX Skyway to base. Over."

"Base to KOTX Skyway. Over. What's up, Randy?"

"Shorty, patch me in to Sheriff Virgil Good, will ya?"

"I happen to know that the sheriff ain't in today, Randy. He'll most likely be out all week. His feet are botherin' him something awful. Of course, they take a powerful beatin' with them three hundred and something pounds weighin' on them all the time. Deputy Jim Howe is fillin' in fer Virgil," Shorty replied.

"Okay, but make it quick, Shorty."

Randy heard a phone ring, an operator answer, "Sheriff's office."

"Bette-Jean, that you? It's Randy Kane up here in the KOTX Skyway. I know Virgil's out with a foot thing, so let me talk to Deputy Jim Howe, will ya?"

"Just a minute, Randy honey," she said.

Deputy Sheriff Howe's voice came booming over the radio. "What can I do you for, Randy?"

"Jimbo, you up on that story about them three Yankee crazies coming down the Miss on a raft with a P-51, headed for God-knows-where?"

"Yeah, what about it?"

"Well, I got 'em in my sights."

"You funnin' me, boy?"

"I'm lookin' at 'em. You want 'em or don't you?" Randy asked.

"I sure do. Where are they?"

"On the river, tied up, cutting brush. Looks like they're tryin' to hide theirselves. They're about a quarter of a mile south of Charlie Faris's place."

"I'm on my way, Randy. . . . Be there in about twenty minutes. Keep your eye on 'em. You done good, boy. I owe you one. Over and out."

Within five minutes the sheriff's office had put out an all-points bulletin and a small armada of police cars converged on the crew of *Earth Angel*. When they got to within a hundred yards of where *Earth Angel* was tied up, the police proceeded on foot with their shotguns and six-shooters at the ready, wearing flak jackets and carrying tear gas. One even carried a machine gun. Approximately twenty-five yards from *Earth Angel*, they stopped behind Deputy Sheriff Howe, a giant of a man with a round head that was balding. What little hair there was left was greasy and curly. His bulging eyes were wild. The big spaces between his square teeth gave him a jack-o'-lantern look. He picked up his bullhorn and cleared his throat into it with the button in the ON position.

The sound startled the crew of *Earth Angel* and all the birds in the trees.

"All right, you suckers. It's all over. This here is

Deputy Sheriff Jim Howe talkin'. You're surrounded. Put up your hands. Drop your guns and come out one at a time. All three of you fugitives is under arrest. If you don't come out in two minutes, we're comin' in shootin'. You got three . . . er, I mean two minutes."

"Let me handle this," Will said to Ben and Jackie. "Morning, Sheriff," Will said cupping his hands to his mouth. "I think there's some mistake. We're not fugitives, and we don't have any guns. But our hands are up. You're more than welcome to come in and see for yourself that we're just tourists . . . just three folks passing through."

"I know who y'all are, all right. You're them three loonies. Fanatics, that's what you are. And you're thieves, too. We're comin' in, but I warn you, y'all try any funny stuff and we'll blast ya."

"We won't move a muscle, Deputy. You can be sure of that. Don't you and your boys get nervous."

"Me and my boys will git anything we want to git. Don't go tellin' us what to git or not to git. If we want to git nervous, we'll git nervous."

The deputy and his men advanced slowly, with guns drawn and the safeties off. They circled Will, Jackie, and Ben. "All three of you are under arrest," he said.

"What's the charge?" asked Jackie defiantly.

"Got a long list of charges, but mostly stealin' and bein' crazy."

"We haven't stolen anything, and since when is being crazy a crime?" Jackie shot back.

"Add talkin' back to the actin' sheriff," he said, "and stealin' this here airplane. And add trespassin' on the Faris ranch and unlawfully cuttin' his brush—destroyin' his property. You folks gonna go away for a long time, and we gonna be all over the TV for a long time."

He gestured to the man nearest him to start handcuffing the three Yankees. "This here's Deputy Sharkey Peel. And he can be real mean, so don't do anything to cross him."

Seconds later Will, Ben, and Jackie were handcuffed and shackled by Deputy Peel. That done, Deputy Howe, standing ten feet from *Earth Angel*, took out a lasso, twirled it over his head, and easily roped the propeller. Will Wright winced at the sight of that.

"Good ropin', Jimbo. You ain't lost yer touch," said Sharkey.

"'Jumbo' would be more like it," grumbled Jackie. "He's got an ass like an elephant. What a piece of—"

Jackie stopped in midsentence at the sight of Jimbo Howe climbing up on *Earth Angel* and straddling the cowling between the cockpit and the propeller. Ben looked away in disgust as Howe shouted, "Yippee! Hey, someone git a pitcher of this."

"Git a pitcher of *this*," said Jackie under her breath mockingly, pointing to her own rear end. The three of them were shoved into the back of the sheriff's car, with *Earth Angel* in tow.

CHAPTER EIGHTEEN

Before the Bar of Justice

Jails are generally ratty places, and this one was no exception. It had bars, of course; a filthy sink in one corner; a leaky, stained toilet without a seat; a jailhouse smell; and two bunks, each with a two-inch mattress, hinged to the wall and held up by heavy chains.

There were a lot of dirty words written on the dirty walls, most of which had to do with Sheriff Good and Deputy Howe. From the barred window, they could see *Earth Angel* in the parking lot below. Within an hour, the word got around town that Jimbo Howe had captured the three desperadoes the whole country was looking for. Will was worried that they would let the kids climb all over *Earth*

Angel or try to take some of her parts for souvenirs. He was relieved when he saw Deputy Peel placing yellow tape all around the plane, even though the tape read CRIME SCENE—DO NOT DISTURB. Again Will winced at the treatment given to this public and private monument—Will's hope of preserving both a fine example of American ingenuity and those special times spent with Casey.

"You Yankees are gonna get a chance to tell your story to Judge Harvey Wade Bench, otherwise known as the Hangman—a real, honest-to-God hangin' judge," said a grinning Deputy Howe as he stuffed an entire chocolate doughnut into his mouth.

With teeth like that he should never smile, thought Ben. And with a body like that he should never eat another doughnut. "Havin' met the deputy sheriff, I can't wait to see the judge," Ben said aloud.

"Take it easy, Ben," said Will. "That kind of talk won't help us out of this."

After an hour or so, the three were led out of the cell and shackled together once again, this time for the trip across the street to the courthouse. Once there, they slowly made their way into the courtroom of Judge Harvey Bench. Only Judge

Bench wasn't sitting that day; he was off hunting cougar, and Judge Martha Bird was presiding.

Judge Bird was a black woman in her mid-forties, attractive, stern looking, and definitely all business. She barely glanced down at the three as they were led in and placed in front of her.

"What is the complaint here, Deputy?" she said.

"Judge, I want to hold this hearin' over until tomorrow, when I understand Judge Harvey Wade Bench will be back from up-country. If I'd of known that you . . . er, that he was off today, I never would of brought these three—"

"Well, I'm afraid you're stuck with me, Deputy, so we'll both make the best of it. Now, we'll start again. What is the complaint?"

"These are the three fruitcakes been on TV, in all the newspapers, and everythin'. You must have—"

"I asked you what the charges are, Deputy, not for your medical, psychological, or editorial opinion. Let's start again. For the third time now, what is the charge?"

Scowling and loudly clearing his throat, Deputy Howe said, "Transportin' stolen property and trespassin' on the Faris place this mornin', er, Your Honor."

"Is that all of it?"

"No, ma'am! This is also a case of unlawfully cuttin' down some brush—destroyin' property and talkin' back to a law enforcement officer. These three old Yankee weirdos here—"

"Deputy Howe," Judge Bird said, interrupting, "is there anything else?"

"Ain't that enough, for God's sake?" Deputy Howe shot back.

Judge Bird ignored Deputy Howe's sarcasm and impertinence and for the first time addressed the three directly. "Gentlemen and Madam, are you represented by counsel or do you wish to speak in your own defense against these charges?" Will stepped forward, which meant they all had to step forward because they were still joined at the hip and ankle. "Your Honor, we are not represented by a lawyer, and I would like to speak, since I'm the one who got both of these two fine people into this."

"Very well," she said. "Please state your name for the record, and let's hear your side of it."

"My name is Wilbur Wright, and that plane in the parking lot is what this is all about. She is a war hero just as much as any man or woman who fought valiantly for this country. This is a plane that helped end a terrible war fifty years ago. She belongs to history, and she deserves a better future than what's in store for her. We're on our way to find an engine for her so we can fly her somewhere. We'd like to give her to some air museum. Chances are they'd put her on display for a lot of people to see. . . . Future generations of Americans will be able to see her and treat her the way *Earth Angel* deserves to be treated. There are some private reasons too, Your Honor, but that's basically what this is all about."

Judge Bird spoke directly to Will. "I know some of the details of your story, Mr. Wright. Dan Rather—who happens to be a son of Texas—had a piece on the *CBS Evening News* several nights ago. There have also been two or three wire-service stories in the newspapers about you, and even a few reported sightings of your raft. Do you three know that you have successfully evaded the entire southern command of the U.S. Coast Guard, the Louisiana, Mississippi, and Texas Air National Guards, Mr. Sky King, and—"

"But they couldn't get away from Deputy Sheriff Jim Howe and his men," Howe couldn't help saying.

"Deputy, please try to control yourself," said Judge Bird before continuing her lecture. "And by avoiding capture by these various law enforcement agencies, you have caused them considerable embarrassment, not to mention expense."

"We're sorry, Your Honor. We really are very sorry for putting a lot of people to a lot of trouble and for causing them any embarrassment or expense, but we just couldn't allow ourselves to be caught and run the risk of not being able to finish our mission or even having it delayed. . . . You see, our friend Jackie here is—"

"Yes, I am aware of the fact that Jacqueline Larson has a health problem."

For the first time since they had been arrested, Jackie spoke up and said, "Your Honor, excuse me for correcting you, but I don't have a health problem. I have a health crisis, and if you don't let us go on our way, I'm likely to have it right here in your courtroom."

"Your Honor," bellowed a red-faced Deputy Sheriff Howe, "I recommend we cut the bull—er, cut the pussyfootin' around and hold these here three fugitives in the county mental hospital for thirty days' observation and then turn 'em over to the FBI."

"Your Honor, thirty days is a life sentence for me," Jackie said.

The judge didn't reply. She was studying the faces of the three fugitives.

Jackie noticed that Judge Bird's gaze lingered on Ben's face for a few seconds longer than on the others, and wondered why.

Finally, the judge said, "Before I rule on this case, I would like to see Exhibit A, so to speak, this *Earth Angel* of yours. The court will recess for twenty minutes while the accused and I go out to the parking lot to examine this important piece of evidence." Again she looked at Ben for a moment longer than at the other two, this time taking in his calloused hands in the shiny handcuffs, the chains at his ankles. She added, "And, Deputy, remove those foolish handcuffs and chains and wait here until we get back."

"No, ma'am," said the deputy, "I can't let you do that." Judge Bird stared him down and, after a few seconds, Deputy Howe continued, "Well then, don't blame me if they get away and take you with them as a hostage. You don't know what you're dealing with, girl—I mean, Your Honor."

Deputy Sharkey Peel slowly removed the handcuffs and shackles while Deputy Howe looked on, helpless and unhappy.

Judge Bird led the crew of *Earth Angel* out to the

parking lot, asked a few routine questions, and began to circle the plane. As she walked around it, she reached out and touched it in much the same way that Ben had seen Will do that first night in the barn and many other times since they'd left Rockport. Ben watched closely as she ran her fingers—long, smooth, deep-black fingers—over the propeller edges and the wing tips and over the blue-trimmed silvery skin of the plane. He found his thoughts straying. Did the absence of a ring on her finger mean . . . ? What would those hands feel like—He jerked his thoughts back to the present. Whatever was happening to him? He was here as a prisoner, and besides, since the day he'd let so many women die at My Lai, he had not allowed himself to even dream of tenderness.

Will and Jackie, too, could see that Judge Bird felt the plane was something special, but how that would translate to her handling of the charges against them was something else again. She stood in front of them for what seemed like a long time before she spoke.

"I've seen enough, and I must say I'm sympathetic . . . even moved . . . by your story and by what you're trying to do. But, frankly, laws have been broken and I must do my duty."

Back inside her courtroom, Judge Martha Bird buttoned up her black robe as she mounted the bench. She rapped her gavel twice and declared that court was back in session. "The charges before this court are transporting stolen property, trespassing, and unlawful destruction of private property. These are serious charges in any state, but especially so in Texas, where property rights and privacy are sacrosanct.

"With regard to the stolen property charge, I see no evidence of the fact that the plane is stolen. No stolen vehicle report has been filed, there is no formal complaint, nothing. Therefore that charge— the most serious of the charges—is dismissed.

"But there's no denying that laws have been broken in Texas, and those infractions must be punished. Therefore it is the judgment of this court, taking into consideration that this is a first offense, that a fine of one dollar for each count be leveled against these defendants. If each of you has the two dollars the court is fining you, you can pay it to the clerk of court on your way out. And if you don't have the two dollars in cash, we will accept your personal IOUs and you can owe it to us.

"In any case, you are free to go. You have the good wishes of this court and the state of Texas. On a personal note, I wish each of you every success and Godspeed—with emphasis on speed." With that, she rapped the gavel sharply, declared that the case was closed, and stood up.

Deputy Howe, red-faced and out of control, shouted, "Girl, you can't let them walk out of here. I mean, ma'am, you can't let them walk out of here."

"Yes I can, Deputy, and I am. And you are out of order."

"There's another charge," he said desperately. "Operatin' an improper vehicle. It's unlawful to operate an airplane on a public road in this state."

"Deputy Howe," Judge Bird shot back, "this court is getting weary of your outbursts, your inappropriate comments, and your obvious prejudice against these three people. I'm going to warn you just one more time. If there are any further outbursts, I'm going to hold you in contempt. If you don't think I will, just try me. As to the latest charge, however, that these people are operating an airplane, let me just say for the record, since it has been raised by the deputy, that at the moment *Earth Angel* is not an airplane. Airplanes, by definition, fly through the air. This vehicle cannot fly. She is simply a wide load on the highway, and there's no law against an oversized load as long as it carries a sign to that effect—which she does."

Deputy Jim Howe, looking confused and angry, sat down muttering. Judge Bird ignored him and said to the defendants, "After you settle up the matter of your fine with the clerk of court, I would like to see you in my chambers for a few minutes before you go on your way."

They paid their fines quickly and were ushered into the judge's chambers, where in answer to her question, they told her their destination. Judge Bird responded by saying, "There are a lot of men like Deputy Jim Howe, especially between here and Apache Mountain. Jimbo's not a bad man, he's just a stupid one. This could happen to you again, and frankly, next time you might come up against a judge who sees things the way Jimbo does and you might be subjected to further delays or worse.

"As a district court judge, I have the power to order the Texas Rangers to protect anyone under the jurisdiction of this court. That's precisely what I'm going to do in your case. They will speed you on your way—perhaps help make up for some lost time—and protect you from any Jim Howes out there. They will escort you across the entire state of Texas, right up to this side of the New Mexico border. From there, you're on your own."

Judge Bird then turned and looked directly at Ben and said, "Mr. Mapes, you have been silent throughout this entire proceeding—in the court-room, in the parking lot, and here in my chambers. I've heard from Mr. Wright and Ms. Larson but nothing from you. Have you anything at all to say?"

"No, Your Honor, except that I'll never forget you and what you did for us today. We've had a lot of obstacles to overcome along the way, but this one today could have done us in if you'd been a judge like the deputy sheriff is a sheriff. It would have been all over right here. Now we know that in a few days it will either all come together for us or it won't. That's all I can think about right now, Your Honor. I'm sorry, but I don't have anythin' more eloquent to say except thank you."

Judge Bird looked at Ben again for what seemed like a long time. This time Jackie wasn't the only one to notice; Will noticed it too. Finally, she said quietly, "Thank you, Mr. Mapes. You've actually said quite a lot and you've said it very well. Godspeed, my friends."

CHAPTER NINETEEN

The Stone That Fell to Earth

A half hour later the crew of *Earth Angel* topped off her fuel tanks at the Texaco station and was back on the road heading west along with the armada of Texas Rangers ordered by Judge Bird. In the lead was Ranger Joe Garcia on a Harley-Davidson motorcycle that had a full-sized, elaborately carved, realistic-looking chestnut brown horse's head mounted on the front of the handlebars. The horse's black mane stood out straight in the breeze. On the rear of the Harley was the other end of the horse, complete with a thick black tail. Behind the lead motorcycle were two cars labeled TEXAS RANGERS. Behind the cars were *Earth*

Angel and her crew, and behind them were two more cars. Another motorcycle took up the rear. The motorcycle riders sat on fancy western saddles complete with stirrups, cowboy boots, spurs, and of course, their traditional cream-colored ten-gallon hats instead of helmets.

The caravan streaked across the Texas highways, heading west, following the setting sun at speeds the crew of *Earth Angel* never imagined were possible, stopping only for refueling and meals.

They rode all night and into the next day. At about four o'clock Ranger Garcia raised his left arm above his head, signaling for a stop, and the caravan pulled off on the shoulder of the highway. They couldn't see it, but they knew that a few days ahead of them, off in the distance, was Apache Mountain. Jackie could feel the lump in her throat as she approached the state line. New Mexico held the mountain that had come close to killing her almost fifty years before.

"This here's as far as we go," said Captain Clem Cullum, emerging from one of the cars. "You folks gonna be all right?"

"We will, Captain. And thank you," said Will.

"You folks be careful now, you hear? This is tough country. Rattlesnakes, mountain lions, freezing cold nights, hot days. The desert is killing country. Nothing much lives out here. Nothing much wants to. Lots of men have died out here."

"We don't plan to die here, Captain," said Will. "We'll be here just a couple of days and then we'll be moving on."

"A coupla days is all it takes. I'll say it again: you folks be careful. The other rangers and I have grown very fond of you folks in the last day and a half. You three are good people. We were proud to ride with you and be of service. A lot of people all over the country are pullin' for you, so don't let them and us down by doin' somethin' like gettin' snakebit or somethin' and dyin' out here."

"We'll try not to," said Ben.

Captain Cullum looked at Ben and said, "My God, I almost forgot. Judge Bird handed me this and told me to give it to you when we got to the border. Said if anything happened to it . . . like if I lost it or forgot to give it to you, I should just keep heading west." Captain Cullum handed Ben an envelope.

As he took it, Ben could feel something bulky inside.

The rangers saluted smartly, and a minute later they were headed back in the direction they had just come from. The crew of *Earth Angel* would miss them.

Ben opened the envelope. In it was a handwritten letter and a small leather case attached to a thin leather thong.

Ben began to read the letter to himself but got a few lines into it and said, "I'd like to read this out loud. It concerns all of us."

He began:

Dear Ben Mapes,

My great-grandfather was a slave, as was his great-grandfather, Jama Buto, who was brought to this country from Africa over three hundred years ago.

The story that has been handed down through generations of my family is that as he was being herded onto the ship, he reached down and picked up a small, black, jagged stone because he wanted to take a piece of his native land with him as a reminder of the land he loved and the people he left behind.

Buto means bird in his language, and so Jama Buto became James Bird in this country. He carried the stone in a pigskin sack around his neck and close to his heart because it made him feel closer to the African land and the family he left behind.

Later he came to believe that the stone had special

powers from God, which helped him to endure all manner of pain and suffering inflicted upon him throughout his life. It remained next to his heart until the day his proud but lonely heart stopped beating. The stone went to Jama's son, and when he died, to his son, and then it reached my great-grandfather.

It was next to my great-grandfather's heart the day Abraham Lincoln signed the Emancipation Proclamation, which set him and millions of other slaves free, and which left countless millions of other still-to-be-born black Americans free to pursue the American dream and to participate fully in this wonderful country. When he died, the stone went to my grandfather and remained next to his heart throughout his life. It was with him in the trenches in France during World War I.

It was next to my father's heart when he married my mother and throughout his life—from the jungles of Iwo Jima to what he said was the happiest day of his life, when he saw me graduate from Yale University Law School. The stone was with him years later—in fact, it hung around his neck just weeks before his death— when he saw me sworn in as the first black female dis- trict court judge in the state of Texas.

Many generations of my family believed that the stone gave them strength and courage and had special powers. My sophisticated friends and colleagues would laugh at me if I told them that I, too, believe the stone has special powers, so I simply don't tell them.

After my father died, since there were no sons, I have worn the stone around my neck, next to my heart. It has never been out of my sight, much less out of my possession. A geologist friend at Yale examined the stone and told me that it is actually not from our Earth; it's a piece of tektite—a meteorite fragment that fell to earth from outer space. That makes it all the more mysterious and magical.

When I heard your three stories—Will's, Jackie's, and yours—and evaluated your chances for success, I decided that you would need every extra bit of help possible. And I thought of my little black stone with its special powers.

As you can see, it is no longer the jagged stone it was when Jama Buto picked it up on that West African beach. It has been worn smooth by the flesh of many generations of my ancestors and made shiny by centuries of their sweat and their tears and, yes, even their blood. The time has come for our family to share the stone with another family of three strangers who have come together to join on a noble quest.

And so I place my priceless treasure in your care, Benjamin Mapes, and along with it comes my special prayer that you and Will and Jackie will accomplish your mission. That you all will survive and that you will reach your goal and that you will live happily ever after. That is my favorite phrase in the whole world . . . to live happily ever after. What a wonderful thought that is! I often wonder who first wrote it.

You are all good people—people of character—in a world made up of far too many mean-spirited and venal people. I am intrigued by people like you and Will Wright and Jackie Larson—each as different from the other as three people can be, but yet united together in a common purpose. I am intrigued by men and women who have a passion for someone or something and are willing to risk everything for what they believe in. Being willing to risk the ridicule of others, to the ultimate of risking one's life, is a very noble thing in a world generally lacking in nobility.

You and Will and Jackie love Earth Angel and want to make her whole again and give her a good life. You love your country, too, and you have each served your country. You love one another. You have taken a bold step. You have overcome many obstacles. These are important lessons for us all—particularly our young people. You have inspired those who have heard your story. So you three must succeed, not only for your own sakes and the sake of Earth Angel, but also for the sake of the thousands of Americans who are watching you, learning from you, and praying for you.

Sincerely,

Martha Bird

No one said anything when the last words were read. After a while Ben opened the pigskin leather case and passed the small, smooth, black stone first to Will and then to Jackie. Jackie handed it back to Ben, who put it back in its leather case and put it over his head and around his neck. . . . Tomorrow, the desert and Apache Mountain.

CHAPTER TWENTY

The End of the Road

It wasn't much of an airfield. It didn't even have a name. Then again, there wasn't much need for much more of an airfield in this part of the country. They parked *Earth Angel* next to a twelve-by-eighteen construction trailer marked ADMIN-ISTRATION BUILDING and went in. Inside was Red Martin, the thirtyish owner and manager of the airfield and the pilot of that dusty, faded blue Cessna 180 parked outside.

Will began to explain who they were, but Red Martin interrupted him, saying, "I know who y'all are—the TV and papers have been full of what you're up to. I never expected you'd show up in these parts. I—"

Since they'd been jailed, Jackie's physical condition had deteriorated. Her breathing had become labored again, and her pallor worried Will and Ben. She had also become increasingly impatient and concerned about time. She interrupted Red, saying, "I'm about to tell you the part you don't know anything about, cowboy, and why we're here. In 1943 I was ferrying a P-51 Mustang like the one parked outside from Detroit to San Diego. I decided to do a few fancy steps at about twelve thousand feet, just a few miles north of where we are now. I put her into a spin. After a few corkscrews, when I was at about five thousand, I decided it was time to get her out of the spin. I gave her right aileron and opposite rudder. The moment I kicked the rudder, I felt and heard the elevator cable snap. I began falling out of the sky at a terrible rate of speed."

Red Martin winced and muttered under his breath, "Jeez! How come you're still here to talk about it?"

"You get the picture. I tried everything, and nothing worked. I was just waiting to hit when, by some miracle—and I mean miracle—she pulled out of it by herself and leveled off at around eight hundred feet. But right ahead of me was this mountain. I obviously couldn't go over it and I couldn't go around it. Somehow I was able to set her down in the sand, wheels up, on what I later learned was the western side of Apache Mountain. There was some body damage, so I did another stupid thing. I began burying her. Why I did it is a long story, and I don't have time for long stories. The point is, she's still out there somewhere. We're here because we have to dig her up and see what shape her engine is in to see if we can put it in *Earth Angel*."

"What's all this got to do with me?"

"We want you to take us up and recreate . . . Jackie's flight," said Will. "We want you to approach the mountain from the same direction Jackie did and bring it down to eight hundred feet just like Jackie did and continue on down—"

Interrupting, Red Martin said, "Don't tell me . . . let me guess. Continue on down until I crash, right? And then you'll know exactly where to dig."

"Not exactly," said Jackie. "We want you to continue on down and we'll mark the route with flour bags that we'll throw out of the plane, and at the last minute, just before—"

"Just before I stall out and crash."

"At the last minute," said Jackie, ignoring Red's

comment, "you give her full power and pull her up and—"

"And pray that I don't hit that mountain in front of me."

"At that instant we're gonna drop a balloon full of red ink and, the way I figure it, we should be within a hundred yards of where she's buried," Jackie said.

"You people really are crazy," said Red. "You want me to take you three up in my little plane—which already puts us in the over-gross-weight category—then take her in like I'm gonna make a landing on the desert sand while you throw out flour bags and a balloon full of colored ink. Then, when you tell me to, I put the throttle of my little overweight, underpowered airplane to the fire wall and expect her to pull up, narrowly missing Apache Mountain."

"Precisely," said Jackie. "You are a quick learner."

"Jeez! You're pilots. You know that everything's gotta be just right—the wind, the weight, the engine response, everything. One miscalculation, one missed cue, one sputter of the engine, and we could all get killed. Is it worth dying for?"

"It is to us," Jackie said. "It will be to you, if you're the pilot I think you are. But if you don't want to chance it, we understand and . . . no hard feelings, just lend me your plane. I'll do it myself and I promise I'll bring it back to you without a scratch on it."

"How much time do I have to think about it?" asked Red, shaking his head.

"There are some times in life when the longer you think about somethin', the less you're gonna want to do it," said Ben. "This is definitely one of those times. But another thing Jackie forgot to mention is this black stone around my neck. It has special powers . . . it won't let anythin' bad happen to us."

"Oh, that makes me feel a lot better," said Red. "Why didn't you folks tell me about that magic stone right from the start? Yes sirree, that makes all the difference in the world."

Red Martin looked away for a moment, wondering what it was that made him want to be part of this adventure. He shook his head, then said, "We should take off at first light when the air is cool and before the thermals build up. So be. . . ."

At five o'clock the next morning, the four climbed into the small plane and took off. It was good to be in the air again. Except for that brief liftoff over the covered bridge, it had been a long time for Jackie—longer for Will. Jackie was in the right-hand seat and Will and Ben were jammed into the back. When they reached two thousand feet, Jackie said, "Red, I was coming in from the east on a heading of two hundred thirty degrees and I was probably about three miles from the base of the mountain, so move over about fifteen degrees, then take her down to fifteen hundred and do a couple of figure eights so I can get my bearings."

Red followed Jackie's command, and the altimeter wound down to 1,500 feet and the compass needle spun around and settled at the 230-degree mark. The plane started its slow figure eights, and after a minute or so, Jackie said, "Okay. Yeah, that's about right. Now, line up your nose with the mountain, and start to drop at a rate of about four hundred feet a minute."

"That means in about three and a half minutes we're either gonna drill ourselves into the ground or splatter ourselves along the side of the mountain," said Red.

"Trust me, cowboy. Just do what I tell you. Trust me."

Red still didn't know why, but he followed Jackie's orders.

As the altimeter of the plane started to wind down once again, Jackie said, "All right, you guys in the back, when I tell you to drop them flour bags, drop 'em. Who's got the red ink balloon?"

"I have," said Ben.

"And do you also have your lucky charm, Ben?" asked Red sarcastically.

"When I holler 'red balloon,' drop it, Ben. Drop it at that instant. Drop it right straight down. Don't throw it, just drop it."

"But be careful not to drop your lucky black stone," said Red, holding his breath.

The plane continued its downward slope, with the ground coming up closer to meet it and the mountain in front of them getting nearer, almost filling the windshield.

Suddenly Jackie said, "Now! Drop the first flour bag. Drop another. Drop another. Drop another. Another. One more. Stand by, Ben. Red balloon is next."

By this time the altimeter was down to 200 feet ... 150 ... 100 ... 75. ... The shrill beep of the stall-indicator alarm sounded continuously—a sound like no other. When it goes off, signaling that the plane is losing lift, a cold hand squeezes the heart of every pilot. A stall in an airplane is not like stalling in a car, where a stall simply means it's time for a tune-up. In a plane, a stall means that the wings cannot keep the plane in the air any longer.

When a stall is imminent, the pilot's training tells him he must add power and keep the nose down. His instinct tells him to pull back on the stick—the wrong thing to do. Red Martin had to resist the strong urge to ignore the sick old woman next to him and take control of his plane to avoid the dreaded stall, but his faith in Jackie held for another thirty seconds, and suddenly he heard Jackie shout, "Now, Ben, drop the red balloon. Red, full power! Take her up, cowboy."

In the next ten seconds Red was too busy to wonder if the command had come too late to save them from crashing. The plane strained to gain altitude, but the force of gravity, which had lost one recent contest with Jackie over a covered bridge, wanted to pull the Cessna down. It was a test of machine over nature.

For a few seconds the plane leveled off but refused to climb, and the stall indicator was still screaming. The landing gear clipped a tall cactus plant and the prop wash kicked up a plume of sand directly in front of the plane, engulfing it so they had no forward visibility. But they didn't need to see in order to know that three hundred yards away, directly in front of them, was Apache Mountain.

Even Will braced himself for what seemed to be a certain crash because they had taken ten seconds too long and he knew it. Ben, his eyes shut, was gripping the black stone in his hand. Suddenly, as if it had been picked up by some giant hand, the blue Cessna began to climb. It went from 25 feet to 50, to 75, and then to 100, where it barely made it around the lowest point of Apache Mountain.

Jackie, obviously loving every terrifying second, let out a loud yell as she slapped Red on the back. "Good job, cowboy. I'd fly with you any day."

Will took a deep breath.

The color began to come back into Red's face around the same time Ben opened his eyes and released his death grip on the black stone, saying, "One save for the Bird stone."

Red did not object. He was feeling good now . . . very good. In fact, he couldn't remember when he'd felt as good as he was feeling at that moment.

CHAPTER TWENTY-ONE

The Burial Ground

Once back on the ground, the thank yous and back slapping over, the talk turned to paying Red.

"I'll settle for a ride in her," he said, pointing to *Earth Angel*. "Just let me know when she's ready." He headed for the trailer that served as his office, weather station, and living quarters.

The three climbed back on *Earth Angel* and with Jackie in the cockpit taxied to where the flour bags and the red-ink balloon had landed. They drove four stakes into the sand and marked the area off with clothesline. It was roughly the size of a football field, and in the center was the large red stain on the sand. Leading the way to it were the splotches of white flour about every twenty-five feet.

Holding the Sears metal detector, Will said, "Too bad we could get only one of these, but it's better than having to dig up the whole field."

"She's out there somewhere," said Jackie. "I know she is. I can feel her close by. I can feel it."

"Why don't we start at the red marker and work our way back?" Will suggested.

"No. I think we should start at the red marker and work our way forward," Jackie said. "I think I was actually a little closer to the mountain when I touched down."

"Closer?" said Ben. "If you were that close to the side of the mountain, then you really should have died fifty years ago. You've been livin' on borrowed time all these years."

The three moved onto the roped-off area with the metal detector and three shovels. After three hours there was nothing, and they were starting to wilt in the noonday sun. An hour later they were well down the field—if it had been a football field, they would be past the fifty-yard line, almost at the forty—when suddenly the needle on the metal detector started reacting violently in Ben's hands. He called to the others a few yards away.

"It's here! It's here! Right here!" He pointed to a spot in the sand.

Will and Jackie started digging, and Ben got down on his knees and began tearing at the sand with his hands. Moments later Jackie's shovel hit something—the unmistakable sound of metal on metal. They dug furiously in that spot. Suddenly Ben, who was still digging with his hands, yelled, "Stop! It's a bomb! Back off. Just . . . back . . . away."

Will and Jackie did what Ben commanded.

In the silence, with his hands, Ben gently cleared the packed sand away from the bomb. A few seconds later he uncovered the impact detonator fuse on the nose of a 600-pound, high-explosive bomb. His voice barely a whisper now, Ben said, "It's one of those impact fuses. Nose up. . . . It never exploded when it was dropped here because it landed tail-fins first in the soft sand. Over the years it got covered over, I guess."

His words were greeted by more silence. Will looked pale and exhausted.

When she was able to breathe again, Jackie said in wonder, "It could have exploded when I hit it with the shovel."

"That's right, it could have," Ben agreed, "but it didn't. That's two saves in one day for the Bird stone . . . one up there, one down here."

"They must have used this area during the war as

a practice range. God knows how many of those things are around here. We'll have to be more careful," Will said.

Ben drove a stake into the ground a few feet from the bomb and tied his red handkerchief to it. For the next hour the three continued their search with the metal detector. They didn't find any more bombs, but when they got down to about the ten-yard line, Will, who was now operating the metal detector, called out, "I've got something."

They looked at the needle and then at each other. No one spoke a word.

They started digging very carefully this time, using just their hands. Ben was the first to feel it. He slowly sank his hands deep into the sand, feeling for what it might be, and shouted, "It's a prop! It's the edge of the prop."

Jackie got down beside Ben. "Show me where it is. Let me feel it. No, it's not the prop, but it is my plane! It's the tail. It's the leading edge. It might feel like the prop to an infantryman, but it isn't. I always said infantrymen don't know their—" She thought better of finishing what she had started to say.

All three of them started pulling at the sand. Within a couple of minutes they uncovered about twelve inches of the tail section, complete with its World War II paint and markings. They were wildly excited. They had come a long way for this moment. But they still had a long way to go, and they knew it.

"We don't have to take all of her out," Will said. "As a matter of fact, we should leave her buried. All we have to do is measure the distance from the edge of the tail to the prop on *Earth Angel* and do the same here and start digging from the other end. We can probably save ourselves a day or more of digging."

They took the measurements and started digging where they thought the prop should be. It wasn't long before they uncovered it. Then the cowling. And then the cockpit bubble. They removed enough sand so that the entire front end and left side of the plane that had been buried for all these years was now fully exposed. It was an eerie sight to see the plane emerge from its sandy grave. Jackie's landing had done a lot of damage, and Ben could see that the sight of the twisted metal of the plane's prop and the gashes in her fuselage and tail section had a devastating effect on her.

After two more hours of digging and brushing away the sand, they were ready to open up the cowling and look inside the engine compartment. They carefully unfastened the T-shaped cowling latches. Jackie opened it.

"Amazing," said Will. "Just like the day it was installed. It even smells new."

"All the seals look tight. Even the rubber is still soft," Ben said.

"There's still oil in the crankcase," said Will, sniffing, "and it smells fresh."

"Must have been the combination of the heat, low humidity, and the cool nights," said Ben. "That plus a couple of feet of sand were enough to keep her insulated and dry."

Will looked at Jackie and said, "You did it, Jackie. You found her."

"Yeah, I found her," said Jackie with tears in her eyes. "Look at what else I did. I killed a perfectly good airplane and then buried my mistake. That's what I did. For what?"

"For this, Jackie," said Ben. "For this. Don't you see? It was destined to happen this way. This plane's gonna live again when *Earth Angel* flies."

Jackie said nothing.

They worked all afternoon and into the night, taking out the engine of the half-buried plane, carrying it by hand over to *Earth Angel*, gently setting it down on a tarp. Then they began taking out the old Buick engine. That done, they lowered the new engine into *Earth Angel*. They bolted it to the airframe, hooked up the lines from the fuel tanks, and connected all the systems to the instrument panel.

They began the task of reburying Jackie's old plane, along with the Buick engine that had carried them so far and performed so well for so long. They were burying old friends, and they did so in silence.

CHAPTER TWENTY-TWO

Another Surprise from Jackie

Later that night they huddled around the campfire. Earlier in the evening they'd cooked their meal over it, and now it provided some welcome warmth from the chill of the desert. Each day since they'd left Rockport, and particularly since they'd left Chicago with Jackie on board, the camaraderie between them had grown stronger. This evening everyone was unusually quiet, aware that the journey was soon coming to an end. They had come a long way and were tired and apprehensive about tomorrow. Tomorrow this chapter of their lives would be over, that was certain. What would they do then? What would become of them? What would they go back to? They knew only that they could not go back to the same lives they had left behind, nor did they want to.

Jackie broke the silence. She began speaking softly, never taking her eyes away from the flames of the campfire. "That plane out there is not the only one I sent to an early grave. There was another. I think about that one a lot, too. It happened about four months before the end of the war.

"I was assigned as a ferry pilot with the Hundred-and-first Fighter Squadron stationed on Okinawa. We were assigned to escort the B-29s on their daily bombing runs to the Japanese mainland. Escorting those twenty-nines was not my idea of fun. They were slow, they flew high and in formation, and nothing ever happened. The night before one of my scheduled runs, I went out on the town—such as it was—to let off a little steam. I got myself lit up on the local hooch and got back to my quarters at about four in the morning. They got me up an hour later.

"I fell in on the flight line—I should say staggered in—I had a tough time standing. The squadron leader, a guy from Brooklyn named O'Reilly, took one look at me and knew I was in tough shape, but he was short on pilots. That's why I got picked. I guess he decided that once I started sucking on one of those oxygen bottles at twenty-five thousand feet, I'd sober up in a hurry. I remember he confronted me about my drinking and told me he was putting me at the back of the formation where I'd be out of harm's way. That way I didn't have to do any thinking. All I had to do was follow.

"There were twelve of us; three in the front, three in the back, and three on either side of the twenty bombers. The fighters flew in a diamond formation. I was the last plane. I remember taking off last, meeting up with the others, getting into the formation and climbing to our cruise altitude of twenty-five thousand feet, and setting a heading north to Pusan, Korea. From there we would turn east to the Japanese mainland. Once we completed our mission, we were supposed to make a beeline back to Okinawa. If we were lucky, we'd have about a capful of gas to spare and we'd make it.

After we reached cruise altitude, I remember kicking off my flight boots, pushing back the seat, and actually putting my feet up. We were on automatic pilot, so there was absolutely nothing for me to do for the next six hundred miles to Pusan except to occasionally check the instruments to make sure my engine and other systems were okay. Somewhere between Okinawa and Pusan I fell asleep. I don't remember a thing until I felt a tremendous impact that threw the plane fifty or a hundred feet to one side and immediately slowed its forward motion. I woke up in a hurry. My feet were still on the instrument panel. The engine had stopped. The propeller wasn't turning. Just an eerie silence, with the wind whistling around outside the cockpit. I looked ahead, expecting to see the other planes, and there were none. I was alone.

"It was then I realized that the others had made their turn east and I'd just kept flying straight on autopilot. I never heard the squadron leader squawk the turn command on the radio. They were on their way to Japan without me and without that pair of eyes that was supposed to be looking out for enemy aircraft to the rear. I didn't know where I was, but chances are I was somewhere over Manchuria. Then I looked out at the cowling and couldn't believe what I saw.

"There was a giant spear, probably six feet long and three inches round with tail fins on it, sticking into my engine compartment. I was sure there had been no explosion—even asleep I would have heard it. There was no fire. No smoke. Nothing. Just this weird spearlike projectile that had struck the engine while I was sleeping and caused it to stop. I had no idea where it had come from or what it was. Then I saw who had shot it.

"I looked out the left side of the airplane and I saw a Jap Zero not twenty feet away from me. The pilot was just sitting there grinning. I looked on the other side and there was another one smiling at me off my right wing tip. That thing in my engine must have been one of those new rockets we heard the Japs were experimenting with in the closing days of the war. I'll never forget the looks on their faces. They could have finished me off right then, but they knew I was done for and they were playing cat and mouse with me. They wanted to have some fun watching me squirm.

"When I began to get my wits about me, I noticed that I was at twenty-one thousand feet and the altimeter was winding down steadily but very slowly. Just a couple of hundred feet a minute. At that rate and at my altitude, it would take me almost half an hour to plow in. I realized that as I got closer to the ground, or if I attempted to make a landing, the Japs would probably finish me off. All of a sudden I noticed a large cloud bank about two miles directly ahead of me.

"I headed toward it, with the Japs right along

with me—and by now I saw that there were three of them. Just as I headed into the cloud bank, they peeled off—they obviously wanted to stay out of it. They probably figured they'd catch me on the way down or on the other side, but anyway, they disappeared. Once in the clouds, I knew my only chance was to bail out. I'd never jumped before and wasn't looking forward to it, especially with a twenty-five-below-zero temperature out there, but by then, with the engine stopped, it was starting to get very cold in the cockpit. Ice was starting to form on the inside of the cockpit canopy. In another minute or so the canopy might freeze shut.

"I locked her in a slight turn to try to keep her in the clouds and buy myself some time before the Japs saw her and realized I'd left the plane. I tightened the harness on my chute, popped the canopy, stood up in the seat, and stepped out into the cold, wet, gray-black clouds. I remember counting out loud. The chute opened with a jolt that felt like it was going to tear off my arms. I was in the dark clouds, slowly drifting toward earth, when suddenly I heard something coming toward me.

"At first I thought it was one of the Jap planes, but there wasn't any sound of an engine—it was more like a whistle. I could see the rotating beacon of a plane. At first the light appeared small, but as the plane came closer and I could see the wing-tip lights, I knew it wasn't a Jap plane. Seconds later I could see that it was my own plane coming right at me.

"It passed a few feet over my head—I could have reached up and touched it. Then it disappeared back into the clouds. A ghost ship. My own ghost ship. A few minutes later I broke through the clouds. I didn't see the Jap planes and began to think about where I might be landing. Then, suddenly it was there again. My plane had descended out of the clouds right in front of me; it was in a gentle right bank.

"I watched, fascinated in a way, and relieved that it was going away from me, but then it turned in a wide arc on a collision course with me. I panicked. It was coming right at me—this time it was under me.

"I tried to raise myself above it by climbing up the nylon risers, only to have the parachute start to collapse when I pulled on them. The plane was definitely going to come under me, and I remember instinctively pulling up my feet and shouting for it to go away. This time it passed about eight feet in front of me. It was so close I could read the instrument panel as it glided past me and back into the clouds. Once again I started to breathe normally.

"I was beginning to relax a little bit when it made a grand orbit about half a mile in front of me and started back toward me again. By this time I was convinced that it was trying to kill me for what I'd done. To this day, I still think it was. After that third and final pass at me, it started porpoising in the air. I couldn't take my eyes off it, and it was made even more ominous-looking by the brilliant anticollision light that was flicking its eerie beam. The plane suddenly rolled over on its back and fell straight down to earth. I heard it hit with a ripping, tearing noise. Minutes later I hit the ground myself, and eventually made my way back to our lines with the help of some Manchurian partisans."

All the time she was talking, Jackie never looked up from the fire. She spoke in a low voice, almost a monotone, with no trace of either the very ill Jackie Larson they'd first met in the VA Hospital or the tough, confident adventurer Ben and Will had come to know and love in the past two weeks.

"My life has been one irresponsible act after another—one failure on top of another. I failed in the service of my country. I failed in civilian life. I failed in my marriage. But you guys and *Earth*

Angel have given me another chance—and I know it's my last chance. You've given me another shot at doing something useful. You've let me be part of your team—something I could never seem to get right. You gave me an adventure, too, when I thought I'd never have another. You gave me a chance to make things right with Don when I thought I never could. You gave me a chance to have some fun, too, when I thought my fun days were over. You've depended on me and made me feel like I can make a difference.

You've given me a chance at a kind of . . . redemption, I guess."

Will started to say something, but his voice cracked. He cleared his throat and began again. "The fact is, Jackie, we couldn't have come this far without you. Ben and I would not have made it alone. We would have failed—you must know that. We've depended on you, and you've come through. And we're not finished depending on you, because tomorrow you're going to fly *Earth Angel*, and Ben and I are going to be right up there with you."

"Depending on me," said Jackie almost to herself. She slowly looked up from the fire at Ben and Will and said, "My finally coming through for those who need me—for the first time in my life. Two 'saves' as Ben calls them, a redemption for me, and a resurrection for *Earth Angel* all in the space of twenty-four hours. It's enough to make a believer out of me."

Jackie smiled her new, beautiful smile.

CHAPTER TWENTY-THREE

Good News

After that things got very quiet again. Finally, Will turned to Ben and said, "You've been very quiet, Ben. What are you thinking?"

"Oh, just thinkin' about my own demons. Thinkin' about Judge Bird and some of the things she said. Mostly, I'm wonderin' if *Earth Angel* will start, and if she does, will she be able to get up enough speed to take off on this sand? If she does get off the ground, will she fly? Will a cable break? Will a bolt shear? Will the rivets start poppin'? Just thinkin' about stuff like that."

"We'll know tomorrow," said Will. "We have to take this one day . . . one hour . . . at a time. Just like we've been doing since we started out."

Ben turned on the small portable TV set they had bought on their last supply run and said, "Let's see how close they are to us."

As the volume started to come up, Jackie said, "Maybe that's not such a good idea. Maybe it's better if we don't know."

Before Ben had a chance to respond to Jackie, the TV picture snapped on and came into focus. Once again, Dan Rather was at the anchor desk of CBS News in New York.

"The other night in our "Eye on America" segment we reported on the journey of two men and one woman who have spent the last two weeks on an unusual quest. They are looking for an engine for a World War II P-51 Mustang named Earth Angel. *After traveling along the highways and back roads of America, the three floated the plane eight hundred miles down the Mississippi River on a raft. They traveled at night, we've been told, and successfully evaded the U.S. Coast Guard, various state and National Guard units, and the private army of detectives sent out by billionaire Skyros Rexus, the legendary Sky King, who has laid claim to the P-51 and plans to mount it on the roof of his Atlantic City gambling casino, The Sky's the Limit.*

Three days ago, the three of them and Earth Angel

were spotted near Galveston by a Texas traffic helicopter reporter. They were apprehended by the local sheriff and brought before Judge Martha Bird, a Yale-educated judge with a reputation for being smart, tough, and fair. After a hearing, Judge Bird not only freed them for lack of evidence, but sent them on their way with a Texas Ranger escort. We have some video of that convoy taken two days ago by the Skyway Patrol of our affiliate in Odessa, Texas, KODX.

"Wow, they had a camera on us? Look at us. . . . What a sight," said Ben.

Dan Rather continued:

"According to reliable sources, the three and their plane are now somewhere in the desert in New Mexico looking for a P-51 that has been buried for more than fifty years. Meanwhile, for the past week, public opinion has been building against Skyros Rexus and for the three adventurers.

That unique American institution known as Katharine Hepburn is leading a group of protesters holding an around-the-clock vigil in front of the Greek billionaire's Manhattan townhouse. The New York City post office has been deluged with mail, and there is a human chain around his Sky High casino in Vegas. CBS has learned that Wayne Newton has refused to perform there.

CBS has also learned that bookings on Sky King's Olympus Airlines have fallen off by eighty percent and the airline has had to cancel many flights. Finally, CBS News has confirmed that the President has appealed to Mr. Rexus. As a result, Sky King's public relations firm, Hill and Knowlton, has strongly advised him to call off his chase and salvage what's left of his reputation.

Michael Eisner, the CEO of Disney, has offered to build Rexus an exact replica of a P-51 if he gives up his claim on Will Wright's P-51. In other news today, Wall Street's Dow Jones average closed down twenty-three and five-tenths points in light trading. AOL closed at a record high of one-ninety on the news that it. . . . Wait a minute. This just in:

Skyros Rexus has just announced through a spokesman that he is dropping all legal actions against Will Wright and abandoning all claims to Earth Angel. *The spokesman went on to say that Mr. Rexus joins the millions of Americans who wish Mr. Wright and his two friends every success. That's it for all of us here at CBS News. Good night. And a special good night to Captain Wilbur Wright and his crew of* Earth Angel—*Ben Mapes and Jackie Larson—wherever they may be.*

"Well, what do you know," said Jackie. "Who would have believed it?"

"As the official scorekeeper, that makes two saves, a redemption, an upcomin' resurrection, and a minor miracle," Ben said. "We're on a roll!"

The news meant that they no longer had to hide and that the threat of taking *Earth Angel* away from Will was over. They should have been more excited at the news, but they weren't. They could have turned *Earth Angel* around and headed for home in safety, but they didn't. In fact, that thought never occurred to any of them. Kate Hepburn had summed it up: this was a quest, and like every quest, it had obstacles to be overcome, tests to be endured, and mysteries still to be revealed.

Will's thoughts at that moment were of far away and long ago.

"I wish . . . " Will stopped and looked off into the distant sky.

Jackie and Ben knew what he was wishing for. They also knew that what he wished for was not possible. All the near-miraculous things that had happened to them along the way had been within the realm of possibility—every one of them. There was nothing truly supernatural about any of the things that had happened, even though at times it had felt that way. And they were both convinced that miracles had not happened to them—and wouldn't. What Will was wishing for was a miracle.

To fill the void of silence that followed, and to keep Will from having to say anything more, Jackie said, "Well, if ever there was a night to make a wish, this is it. Just look at that sky out there—full of stars."

"Pick one out and make a wish on it, you two," Ben said, "just like we did when we were kids."

The three looked up at the dark, star-filled western sky and each made a wish. At that very moment, one of the stars fell out of the heavens and disappeared beneath the horizon. They all saw it.

CHAPTER TWENTY-FOUR

Wings

The next morning they wheeled *Earth Angel* into position. The sandy surface they had for a runway would be a traction problem, but there was no alternative. Jackie, wearing the wings Don had given back to her, climbed into the forward seat, Will sat behind her in the second seat, and Ben in the small space behind Will. Jackie searched her memory for the various checklist items and called them out loud, hoping that if she missed something, Will would remind her. But she didn't miss anything.

"Brakes . . . set." Jackie pulled up the brake lever. "Master switch . . . on. Rotating beacon . . . on." The beacon came to life and began rotating.

"Electric fuel pump . . . on. Mixture . . . rich. Throttle . . . back. . . . Clear!" she shouted. And then, "Ignition."

Jackie pushed the ignition button. It cranked weakly. She waited a few seconds and pushed it again. Once again it cranked, but would not turn over and start. She did it a third time. A fourth time. A fifth time. With each try *Angel's* battery seemed to get weaker. The tension mounted. There were over nine thousand parts that made up that engine and any one of them could keep it from turning over.

Under his breath Will said, "C'mon, *Angel* . . . don't let us down. You're just a little stiff, but you can do it. Everything's ready; everything's going to be okay."

On the sixth attempt, the propeller made a half turn but still did not kick over. Jackie tried again and there was a momentary sputter and puff of bluish exhaust. Almost. Again. Almost. On the ninth try the engine caught with a roar and the prop began spinning. With the prop turning, Jackie continued her checklist: "Oil pressure . . . up and normal. Ready to taxi into position."

She pulled the teardrop-shaped canopy closed and, for the first time in half a century, *Earth Angel* moved under the full power she was born to have. The plane slowly taxied down to the end of what served as their runway. Jackie made a half turn into the wind to keep the engine cool and resumed her check of all systems. "Holding in position for run-up. Increasing rpm—she's holding together. Check left magneto . . . okay. Right magneto . . . okay. Carburetor heat . . . on. Throttle back. Increase idle. Fuel tanks . . . okay . . . we're taking off on the left tank. Oil pressure . . . normal. Fuel pump . . . on. Engine temperature . . . normal. Directional gyro . . . on. Set altimeter . . . zero-two-eight. Check ailerons . . . okay on the left, okay on the right. Check flaps . . . flaps okay. Check rudder . . . rudder okay. Trim tabs . . . okay. Suction . . . okay. Prepare for takeoff. Here we go!"

Earth Angel slipped and bounced and fishtailed down the sandy runway for what seemed to Ben like a very long time. It was not a pretty sight. At the end of the runway, there was a twenty-foot-high cactus, and just when it looked as though *Earth Angel* was going to run out of runway and hit it, Jackie shouted, "We're up . . . we're flying. She's flying!"

Tears streamed down one side of Will Wright's face.

"Resurrection," Ben said under his breath as he reached for the black stone around his neck.

After a minute or two they reached 3,000 feet and Jackie leveled off. "Hey, you guys, with all of our plans, we never once talked about what we were going to do when we got her up. We've got forty minutes of gas if we just cruise around, half that if we exercise her a little. What'll it be, Captain?"

"Limber her up a bit," said Will, "but remember, it's been a long time for both of you, so don't overdo it."

"Once a hotdogger, always a hotdogger," Ben muttered to himself as he pulled his seat belt a little tighter.

What followed in the next ten minutes was some of the most spectacular flying ever done. *Earth Angel* climbed, rolled over, looped, did spins—even the tricky Immelmann. It was a one-plane air show. Jackie hadn't lost her touch, and neither had *Earth Angel*.

For Will it was a dream come true and more—much more. A lot of Will's life was here in this cockpit: his love of flying, his love of *Earth Angel*, his lifetime of dreams, memories, thoughts of Jan and Casey, and Will's acceptance of the fact that he would never be able to do what he always said he would do, which was to fly with Casey in *Earth Angel*.

Right after the Immelmann turn, Jackie rubbed her eyes and began squinting. "Will, I think that last turn must have made me a little dizzy. I can't seem to focus my eyes. Maybe if I close them for a few seconds it might help clear it up. Take it, Will, will you?"

His first thought was that this was Jackie's way of getting him to hold the stick and actually fly *Earth Angel* for a moment or two. Typical of the kind of thing Jackie would do, he thought. He said, "I've got it, but just for a minute or two." And he flew the airplane—his airplane—for the first time in half a century.

Seconds later Jackie's breath became loud and labored, and Will saw her slump to one side and weakly put her hands up to her eyes as if trying to shade them. "I . . . I can't see anything except that brilliant white light right in front of us. I can't look at it, but at the same time, something keeps stopping me from looking away from it. It seems to be getting closer. What is it?"

"I don't know, but I see it, too. It seems to be closing in on us at a terrific rate of speed," said Ben.

"Close your eyes tight, Jackie," said Will.

"I can't take my eyes off it," she replied. "I think it's going to hit us!"

An instant later the cockpit was engulfed in the blur of white light, the brightest light any of them had ever seen. It bleached out all other color in *Earth Angel*. The three faces of the plane's occupants appeared ghostly. In the next instant, almost simultaneously with the color loss, *Earth Angel* was rocked by the impact of something that either hit the plane or came very close to hitting it. And in another instant it was over. Color returned to the cockpit; the plane stabilized. But the seat where the pilot had been sitting was empty. Jackie Larson was gone.

"My God!" said Ben.

"She can't be—gone," Will said, ". . . but she is!"

Suddenly a voice came crackling through the earphones, saying, "*Earth Angel*, this is *Guardian Angel*. Look off your left wing tip, please."

Startled by the voice, Will and Ben turned and saw a gleaming Phantom jet fighter not more than ten feet off their left wing tip. There were no markings on the plane, but the pilot in the cockpit was wearing an Air Force khaki flight suit and a helmet with a dark Plexiglas face cover that totally obscured his features. The image of *Earth Angel* and Will and Ben were clearly reflected off the jet's cockpit.

Will hesitated for a few moments. Finally, he said, "*Guardian Angel*, this is *Earth Angel*. There are two of us in this aircraft, and we have just experienced. . . . We have a problem. . . . You see—"

The voice from the other plane interrupted, saying, "*Earth Angel*, this is *Guardian Angel*. I know what you experienced and I am also aware of your pilot's physical limitation and your low fuel situation. I am prepared to assist you if you'll accept my help. Over."

Will responded, "*Guardian Angel*, the crew of *Earth Angel* would welcome your help. This is a fine plane, but she deserves a better pair of eyes than I have. Over."

"Roger, Captain, you do indeed have a great aircraft there. As a matter of fact, she's the last of a breed, so we'll have to make sure she lands without incident. And don't worry about that eye. I've got two good ones."

"Ben, that voice . . ." said Will, and then, "*Guardian Angel*, this is *Earth Angel*."

"Yes, *Earth Angel*."

"*Guardian Angel* . . . is that . . . ?"

"Yes, Dad. It's me."

"But . . . you . . . you were . . ."

"Yes, I was, Dad. My life on earth ended in Vietnam, but I'm here with you now. Don't ask me to explain. This isn't the time. Even if I could, there's no way you could understand it now. Just believe that I'm really here. That I'm here so we can fly together this one last time." And then he added softly, "We do come back sometimes, Dad."

At that moment, years of grief, loneliness, and unbearable pain overcame Wilbur Wright. He could not speak.

"We've been with you from the moment you left Rockport, Dad, and I've been with you from the minute you lifted off today. I stayed off to the side so I could enjoy the show. That Jackie's quite a jockey. Actually, I was supposed to make my appearance a little earlier, but all of you were having so much fun I couldn't interrupt. Jackie's time was up about five minutes after takeoff, but I got her a three-minute extension and then another three. They, that is, my Command doesn't like extensions because they tend to throw everything else off schedule. For example, in six and a half minutes I have to be at my next assignment over New York City."

"Assignment?" said Will, who had regained

most of his composure. "New York City is almost three thousand miles away. I don't under—"

"This is what I *do*, Dad. One of the differences, when life on earth is over, is that we don't do things for a living, we do them for the living. I work in planes. A lot of people get in trouble up here, but for some of them it's just not quite their time. That's where I come in.

"I give them a little guidance, you might call it. They don't even know it because they can't see or hear me as you can, but I'm with them just as I'm with you now. You can see and hear me now because, well, you and I are a special case and my Command knew how much it would mean to both of us."

"Were you that white light we saw a few minutes ago?"

"No, that wasn't me, that was Jackie's . . . let's say escort. It makes it easier to have a guide because it can be kind of scary making that trip alone. It's scary mostly because there's so much mystery about dying. Jackie's okay. In fact, she's already there and should be settled in. Let's see if I can raise her and patch her in to you." After a moment Casey said, "I got her. Hold on a second . . . here you go."

"Will? Ben? Can you hear me?" It was Jackie's voice, sounding strong and calm but also very far away, crackling through *Earth Angel* 's old cockpit speaker.

"We hear you, Jackie," Will said. "We don't understand much of what's happened in the past couple of minutes, but we hear you."

"It must have scared you guys," said Jackie. "It started when I was coming out of that last Immelmann. When we first saw the light and I asked you to take over. There was a voice that seemed to be coming from inside me that told me not to be frightened and to relax, and that it was time to give in. I did, and suddenly I was here. I'm sorry to have run out on you guys, and I'm worried about how you're going to land *Earth Angel* with only one eye, Will, but—"

"Don't worry about us," Will said. "We have help up here. We're in good hands."

"I know all about whose hands you're in, Will, and it's wonderful. I'm so happy for you. I'm so happy. . . ."

Once again Jackie's voice came through the static of the speaker. "You know, what I tried to say last night but couldn't was that the last ten days have been the best days of my life. Meeting you both, meeting *Earth Angel*, our mission, traveling down the river, my meeting with Don one last time, our talks, the campfires, the camaraderie . . . I've been the happiest I've ever been and . . . and I just want to say that . . . I love you guys."

"Don't be goin' soft on us now, Ace," said Ben.

"We love you too, Jackie, and we'll never forget you," Will said over the worsening static.

Suddenly, Casey's voice came over the speaker, clearer and more commanding than before. "Wrap it up, you guys. The clock's ticking and your gas gauge is winding down. I just got word that my New York guy is going to need me real soon. You'll know in a couple of minutes how it all turns out, Jackie. Right now, we've got to get moving."

Jackie's voice was sounding farther and farther away and the transmission was beginning to break up again when she said, "Will, when you get back down, tell Don how it happened. Tell him that it was easy for me when my time came. Tell him that in the end . . . at the very end, it's easy for everyone. Living is harder than dying. Tell him what you said last night about you guys counting on me, and that for once in my life I came through. Tell him I'm happy at last . . . really happy. Tell him I love him and I know we'll meet again. And tell him I'm still wearing my wings. Happy landing, partners. Over and out."

Casey's voice, sounding more formal and commanding, said, "I repeat, *Earth Angel*, we must move along."

Ben cleared his throat and spoke to Casey for the first time, saying, "Sounds like you have an important job, *Guardian Angel*, with a lot of folks depending on you."

"It's the best. It's heaven, Ben. That's exactly what it is. That's what it's all about. When it's all over on earth, you get to go to a better place. A place where there is no fear, no pain, no struggling—all the things that are part of life. Best of all, you do what you have always liked to do best, and you get to do it all the time. Nothing ever really dies, it just changes."

"Where do I sign up?" Will asked.

"Not yet, Dad . . . not yet. You and Mom still have a lot of living left to do on Earth, back home. You two have to make up for lost time. You need each other—

"Hold on a minute. A message is coming through to me." After several seconds of silence Casey said, "I've just been told that the High Command has given my New York assignment a new time for their emergency so that we can have a few more minutes to do a few more twists and turns before we bring her down. I've got the time. You've got enough gas, but just barely. What do you say?"

"You up for it, Ben?"

"Of course I'm up for it—this is what I came along for: a trip five thousand feet above the desert, with a one-eyed pilot in his fifty-year-old airplane and an angel on our shoulder. Who wouldn't be up for it?"

For the next few minutes, anyone who might have been watching from the ground was treated to an aerial display like none other. There were reports from several people within ten miles of Apache Mountain who saw one plane that met the description of *Earth Angel* doing aerobatics over the desert. There were no reports of seeing two planes.

But for Ben and Will, it was as if those two planes were competing against each other. One would do something and the other would attempt to "go" him one better. While they were doing their aerial dance, Will wondered about the unmarked fighter he'd seen with the Stearman over Rockport two weeks before, and also, about a year before that, what had seemed to be the same delta-winged jet flying low over Wright's Garage. Could it have been . . . ? He decided to ask Casey about that later, but right now he had to concentrate on following his son's lead.

After a couple of minutes Casey's voice came booming through the speaker. "We always said we'd take her up together someday, Dad. Remember? I used to say, 'Someday, Dad, we'll dig up an engine for her and fly her.' Little did I know then, but that's precisely what the plan was. You guys did dig her up an engine . . . as planned."

"I've thought a lot about those days," Will said hesitantly. "I've always wondered if I made a mistake, teaching you to love flying. Did I push you into something? Was I responsible for—" He could not finish the sentence.

Casey interrupted him anyway, saying, "Nobody on earth is responsible for anything like that, Dad. It all comes from above. Flying was my destiny. I was born to be a pilot, just like you were. You couldn't have stopped me from becoming one if you'd tried. It's all laid out for us long before we are put on earth. Everything that happens to us happens for a reason.

"I hope you'll think about that too, Ben. I'm

sure you know by now that I was the one who exploded over My Lai that day. The scrap of paper that floated up from the rice paddy and into your hand came from my plane—this plane.

"It was all written before I was born on earth. Actually, it was written on the first day of creation. It was part of the grand plan for all of us—to bring us all together—you, Dad, Jackie, me, Mom, Judge Bird, *Earth Angel*. And it isn't over yet . . . there's more to come. You'll see. Everything that happens to us in life—from the smallest thing to the biggest event—happens for a reason and is all part of a plan that's been in place since the beginning of time. Now I really must go."

These words jarred Will and filled him with dread. He was losing Casey once again. No matter what Casey said about how nothing really dies, Will was losing him again.

In his most commanding voice, Casey said, "Okay, gentlemen, your gas gauge is in the red, so let's do it. Dad, do exactly what I tell you to do. It might not look right to you, but do it anyway. Take her down to fifteen hundred feet on a heading of zero-nine-five."

Will had no trouble taking *Earth Angel* down to 1,500 and holding her on the 095 heading. "Fine," said Casey. "Hold her steady and cut back a little on the power . . . easy . . . not too much . . . that's right. Keep the nose up . . . watch your heading, don't let her drift. Now slow to one-twenty-five. Okay, when I tell you to, you're going to turn left ninety degrees on a heading of zero-zero-five. That'll put you on the base leg to what you guys call an airfield."

"Roger," said Will.

"Now start your turn. You're going to make another left; that will line you up with the runway, and I want you to slow down to one hundred. You'll be descending at the rate of two hundred feet per minute. I want you to hold that until you're eight hundred feet off the ground."

For the next sixty seconds Will did exactly what Casey told him to do. Casey continued to talk Will down, saying, "Okay. Good. Now ease back on the throttle . . . keep that nose up . . . okay . . . full flaps . . . pull back on the power—" Casey suddenly yelled, "Pull *up*, Dad! Pull *up! Full power*! You're too high!"

With *Guardian Angel* still at his side, Will gave *Earth Angel* full power and the plane roared back up, narrowly missing Apache Mountain. "What did I do wrong?" Will asked.

"Nothing . . . *I* did! I didn't remember to tell you to compensate for the thermal buildup near the ground this time of day over this hot sand. We'll have to go around again and come in at a higher angle of attack, and you're actually going to have to fly her into the ground to overcome the thermal effect. I can get you down to that point, but when you hit the thermal layer, you're on your own after that."

"You want me to fly her in? I'm half blind, remember?" said Will.

"Well, as a matter of fact, Dad, I pulled a few strings at Command, and you are about to find out that your depth perception is back to normal. You'll still have only one eye, but it will be a super one. In fact, I wouldn't be a bit surprised if you even passed an FAA eye exam, so you and Mom can make up for lost time with *Earth Angel*."

At the mention of Jan, Will wished with all his heart that she could be there with him and Casey. How could he ever explain all this to her? It didn't seem fair that he should meet Casey again without her. And he'd never missed Jan more than he did at that moment.

But now he had to concentrate on landing a plane. Will cleared his throat and said, "Let's do it."

"Okay, Dad, now we have to do it in one pass. Good, you're all lined up. You're about three hundred feet off the ground. You should be feeling the thermal effect any second now. Just keep her on that course and actually fly her through the thermal layer and into the ground. You have about two hundred feet of thermals to get through. That'll take you seven or eight seconds. Ben, you count off for him. Dad, when Ben gets to the count of eight, pull back on the yoke, cut your power and flare, and just roll her out straight as you can and jump on those brakes as soon as you can. You're on your own, Dad."

"I'm starting to feel the thermals," said Will. "Start counting, Ben."

"One, two, three, four, five, six, seven, eight."

With perfect depth perception, Will brought *Earth Angel* back down to earth. He pulled back on the stick just as the wheels touched down and he began to roll down the sandy runway. He applied the brakes with both feet, eased off, then stepped on them again. The plane came to a stop just a hundred feet short of Apache Mountain. As *Earth Angel* came to a stop, *Guardian Angel* roared over their heads and streaked off into the northeast sky. It was out of sight in an instant, but Casey's voice came over the speaker one last time.

"You made it, Dad! You and *Earth Angel* did it

together. A great piece of flying. You just greased her in. I've waited more than a lifetime to see that." And then Casey proved that he'd been with Will longer than Will had imagined, by mentioning something Will hadn't gotten around to telling his son. "Take her back home, Dad. Fly her! And if you ever get into any trouble, just look over your left shoulder, and I'll be there—but for now, it's time to say good-bye."

Suddenly there was silence. The engine was off. Will flipped the master switch and the whir of the instruments shutting down left Will and Ben sitting there in the total silence. Neither said anything. After a while, they unbuckled their safety harnesses, flipped back the canopy, and climbed out onto the wing, squinting in the bright afternoon sun that was beating down on the desert.

Will climbed down from the wing, stroked the still-cool, smooth skin of *Earth Angel*, and draped his arm around her cowling the way comrades-in-arms often do. After a minute or so, Will looked up at the distant sky in the direction that *Guardian Angel* had gone. There was nothing there. Will knew that in a few hours he would be taking off in *Earth Angel* again. He owed Red Martin a ride and would try to explain what happened to Jackie, and, if Red could believe that much of the story, Will would tell him the rest. . . . After that, Will would set course for the San Antonio airport. He would refuel there, pick up a couple of charts, and plot a course to Erie, Pennsylvania, and Jan.

Suddenly he knew that he would be able to explain his distance from her all these years. And that she would understand. Together they would fly to Rockport and live out the rest of their lives—never again to part, no longer sad about Casey or about the years they had wasted apart from each other.

But what about Ben? What would become of this extraordinary man . . . this friend he had come to love? He had not spoken since they'd landed. Will glanced at Ben, who was still perched on *Earth Angel*'s wing. Over the past few days Ben had seemed . . . not exactly happier, but definitely less sad. Solving the puzzle of the message on the paper he'd picked out of the muddy water of the rice paddy accounted for some of the change. And Will felt that Judge Martha Bird's letter and her black stone had also had a profound effect on Ben. But what was next for Ben? Should he return to Rockport? Or continue to drift from town to town?

Will looked out at the vast desert. Suddenly, off

in the distance, something appeared on the horizon. It was just a speck, but it seemed to be coming toward them, getting larger. Will couldn't seem to bring whatever it was into focus. There was too much distortion from the heat rays rising off the hot sand.

Ben was watching it, too.

As whatever it was got closer, they began to be able to make out something that looked like a person. A hundred yards closer, and they could see that it was indeed a person. Closer still, and they could see that it was a woman. Seconds later they both realized that it was Judge Martha Bird. Ben climbed down from the wing of *Earth Angel* and started walking toward her. Then he began to run, and so did she.

Ben and Martha Bird stopped perhaps twenty feet apart and just looked at each other. A long look. He moved closer, and when they were just a few feet apart, Ben took the black stone from around his neck and held it out to the open hand of Martha Bird. Her hand touched his and at that moment Ben realized that his life had changed forever. He saw how his past was past and there was nothing he could do to change it. He could, though, be a man who reached out to others, helping them with their burdens now, in the present, and for the rest of his life. He held on to Martha's hand and looked into her eyes.

Just before he took her into his arms, the tattered piece of paper that had been with him since My Lai slipped out of his shirt pocket unnoticed. Its message, which had puzzled him for so long before it led him to Will and *Earth Angel* and Jackie, and to Casey and now to Martha Bird, was blowing across the desert sand. It caught on a cactus needle momentarily and then was freed by a strong gust of wind. It began floating away, perhaps to where it had come from.

(And they who had learned these truths lived happily ever after.)